A Special Si... Hardback Edition of

MAY DAY

limited to just 60 numbered copies

Emma Coleman

This is number:

MAY DAY

MAY DAY

Emma Coleman

NewCon Press
England

First published in the UK May 2021 by
NewCon Press
41 Wheatsheaf Road,
Alconbury Weston,
Cambs, PE28 4LF

NPN005 (limited edition hardback)
NPN006 (paperback)

10 9 8 7 6 5 4 3 2 1

ISBN:

978-1-912950-88-1 (hardback)
978-1-912950-89-8 (paperback)

Cover layout and design by Ian Whates

Typesetting and editorial meddling by Ian Whates
Text layout by Ian Whates

One

I'd just turned seventeen when the factory went up. Mum had been at home with my little sister, June; Dad had finished his shift at the boatyard and had been halfway down the road when it exploded.

The whole street went, along with the other three streets coming off the armaments factory. Houses obliterated, glass, bricks, metal twisted like sweet-paper wrappings, all of it blasted and scattered. You could see the entire sky.

The bodies – all red and pink and powdered with brick dust – were broken and trapped in the rubble. Stray dogs blown inside out... I only saw it once and all I could think of was my mum, and her telling me, "Everything happens for a reason."

After finding that home had disappeared, I never went back. And if it hadn't been for the lie I'd told, I'd have gone with them.

I met a boy, Albert, and he'd asked me to the pictures. I told Mum I was going for a job at the Lyons house on the corner of Watney Street and she believed me. I guess I told the fib because of my own embarrassment; I knew I was no Hedy Lamarr, and Albert had been the first boy to ask me out, I didn't want Mum making fun of it. I suppose I felt nervous and a bit frightened, I didn't like the thought of Mum knowing just how far my naivety went. In my mind I had become a woman at sixteen but when Albert asked me out, I realised how much of a girl I still was.

Maybe I should've said something to her, she could've forewarned me of a boy's behaviour and sympathise that perhaps it was his first time, too. She could've told me about wandering hands and how to judge my own feelings instead of clenching and staying silent. Mum would've known. And she would've known how to comfort me and how to make me laugh. And she would've marched straight down to Albert Pensey's house and given him a piece of her mind.

She would've done all that.

Albert Pensey, his wet kisses on my face and fumbling hands up my skirt, became insignificant as soon as I ran onto Pageant Road. I grew old in one disbelieving look at where home used to be.

Albert Pensey became as distant a memory as when I played with a rattle.

I didn't have much choice after that and I went to live with my father's sister in Northamptonshire; she'd moved to a fairly large village called Guilsbridge when I was twelve and Mother had been expecting June, but we'd visited Aunt Celia a number of times since. It felt strange and unnatural moving to a place that had no coastline. I'd lived my life on the East coast, and the sound of the sea was now missing. I found myself straining to hear the waves.

I missed and longed for the sound of the boats and of the boatmen calling to one another through their fishing nets, and of the gulls following the gleaming fish, trapped and jumping on the decks.

It took a long while for me not to wake up – just before the break of dawn – startled and heart thumping, woken by the queer lowing of the remaining cows moaning in the Wilsons' barn, and of the shrill crowing of the cockerel made even louder by the quietness of early morning.

He was the last cockerel in the village. I asked Aunt Celia what happened to the others and she replied, "People must eat," and at that point I realised how fortunate we had been to have the coast and as much fish and as many cockles as we wanted.

My aunt had appeared happy to receive me although I knew she never really approved of my mother; she thought her to be a little eccentric, too bold in opinion and forthright in action to be the wife of her darling brother. She believed father should've married someone with money and standing, failing to recognise that her younger sibling was only the skipper of a fair-sized fishing trawler and not a councillor or speaker for the House of Lords.

Mother had always made fun of Aunt Celia and her delusions of grandeur but with a sense of sympathy, she pitied anyone who couldn't see the mysteries in life or revel in the unknown.

She mocked the strait-laced repression of England but would defend it fiercely if anyone else should berate the English sense of place and politeness. She felt she had the right to do so having come from an Anglo-Irish, Austrian-Jewish background; she had an allowance to mock any of these and at the same time swell with pride when speaking of her heritage.

It seems strange that Mother and Father ever married at all.

"We, in this household, go to church every Sunday service without fail," my aunt had announced the day after my arrival and whilst pouring tea in the 'parlour', and even though only myself and my aunt lived in the house. "I know your poor dear parents were rather... relaxed in these matters, shall we say, but here in this house we all of us do our Christian duty."

I understood from the way she had spoken, 'Christian', that she referred to my mother's Jewish background despite the fact she knew very well that Mother had never even seen a synagogue let alone read any Jewish scriptures.

"Of course, Aunt Celia," I had replied politely. "Religion has never been needed as much as it is now. If we all pray hard enough the war might just go away."

I coughed and then reached for my teacup. I knew my meaning wouldn't be lost on her and I watched my aunt's face pinch with disdain. She thought I'd grown too much like my mother and was always offended by the reminder that other religions existed.

I had no interest in faith, but I had read the Old Testament. I enjoyed the stories but with the same enjoyment as when reading the Greek myths. I didn't for one minute think they should be taken seriously and that people should live their lives by them.

Neither did Mother. If we ever had a religion, a way of life, then it would be her superstitions which would guide us and tell us what we could and couldn't do, even though as a ten-year-old, I didn't fully appreciate what she taught me. These superstitions eventually burrowed their way into my bones.

For my mother it was spiritualism rather than religion; her large family had denied their Judaism two generations or more ago, and so the traditions of old wives tales took its place. Something had to fill the void.

Father would always be bemused by us and our ways, but he'd never laugh or tell us that we were being silly. He understood Mum's feelings and respected her strength of character – something, I suppose, that attracted him to her in the first place – and he would remain quiet and smiling whenever Mum read the leaves.

Looking back, I think he must've been grateful for having such a brilliant wife, someone who saw beyond his – as he saw them – physical deficiencies, and clearly loved him for all he was. His lameness of foot prevented him from going to war and this could've gnawed away at any man, making him feel useless and pitiable, but with Mum, this would never be allowed. She buoyed him along throughout life and he forgot his self-pity. He was a strong man and would've worked the boats into his nineties if the war had permitted... Oh, Dad, I still remember the smell of your pipe tobacco and the way you polished your shoes every evening on the kitchen table. Quick, sharp strokes with the brush after smearing a little boot polish in a small circle on the toe with an old rag, your hand stuffed into the shoe and held up to the light, the look of affection and concentration on your face... I don't think you realised that June and I were watching you, both of us smiling at you as you took great care in protecting the leather. Maybe you did.

June, little June, she was the sweetest thing you'd ever seen with her curls of red hair and blue eyes – just like Father's – and she hardly ever cried. She was always happy and full of joy for everything.

Mother had named me May after the month of my birth, and when she found out she'd given birth to another girl, she loved the idea of being able to introduce her two daughters as May and June.

The name never suited her, though.

And so, when I was a child, I'd leave Mother and June in the mornings, waving at them both from the end of the street, June in mother's arms and flapping a chubby little arm about, and make my way to school two miles or so away. And then I'd return, passing the boatyard and calling for Dad if I saw his trawler in, before running the last few streets home. I knew what would be waiting for me when I got in.

Gloves, knives and sometimes a pair of dressmaking scissors, strewn on the floor or nudged under sideboards out of harm's way of toddling June, sitting on the rug and sucking liquorice, pointing at all the things and smiling. She knew even then our mother's ways and laughed at them with love.

"Ooh, May, there you are at last," my mum would say, coming in from the yard and wiping her hands on her apron, "pick up that fillet knife over there. I dropped it this morning when I was filleting that blasted herring and I couldn't very well ask June to fetch it up now, could I? And tea'll be late. I'm all behind what with one thing and another…"

She'd have left them on the floor for days – weeks even – if nobody had come home, and she would've gone through all the other knives and scissors in the house rather than pick them up herself.

"…and there's one of my gloves by the front door, you probably stepped right over it as you came in. Be a good girl and pick it up for me, I had trouble pulling them off when I got back from the grocer's and I practically pulled my skin off with that one. It's the weather, makes my hands swell…"

That and the smell of vinegar, my two most vivid memories of walking in from school; I knew she had cleaned the windows and I've hated the smell of vinegar ever since.

"Vinegar and brown paper, mark my words, gets the glass all bright and clean. You'll understand when you're married."

"Yes, Mother."

"And remember, you mustn't launder on New Year's Day, there's sure to be bad luck following on."

"Yes, Mother."

"Don't you go looking at that new moon through glass. If you want to see it, go and stand in the yard."

"All right, Mother."

"May! You're not mending that skirt while you're still in it? What have I told you? If you haven't got the patience to take the garment off, then you must chew on a piece of white cotton. How many times have I told you?"

"Sorry, Mother, I forgot."

"And while we're on the subject, it's Sunday today, so when you have your wash-down this evening, remember not to cut your toenails. You can do it in the morning. One more night with talons won't hurt."

"Where on earth did those peacock feathers come from?" she demanded one day, her face angry and worried at the same time, "Get them out, get them out at once! What have I told you about the evil eye? Never bring them into the house, *never*."

One of my favourites used to be when I spilled salt and had to take three pinches – one at a time – and flick them over my left shoulder. If I manoeuvred myself well enough, I could get Dad in the face as he read the paper. He always clipped me lightly on the back of the head, but I knew it amused him; it was one of our private moments. If he didn't like me doing it, he would've moved out of the way.

Sundays were the best days, before the war of course. We had tea at four o'clock; bread and butter, boiled eggs, tomatoes and lettuce from the pots in the yard, black pudding and, for afters, jam tarts or maybe a fruit cake if we were lucky. Sunday teatime meant tea-leaf reading. Dad would let Mum read his cup and he'd listen to everything she saw, but as soon as it was over he would completely forget what she'd said.

I, on the other hand, was enthralled and begged Mum to teach me how to do it.

"You pick these things up, May, that's all, you pick these things up. Just listen and learn."

Autumn, if we were able to get apples, would mean divination by skin tossing. Mother and I would sit at the kitchen table and peel the apples. She was so good at peeling an apple in one go and then – quick as a flash and with the knife still between her finger and thumb – she'd toss the skin behind her.

"What does that look like to you, May?"

And I'd look and say, "Maybe an 'M'... or a 'W' from the other way up."

"Go on, girl, it's your turn."

I'd fling my sorry piece of apple skin – no more than two inches long – and stare forlornly at the outcome.

"Oh dear, never mind," Mum would say, chuckling, "it's another 'C'. Not to worry, one day a handsome young man called Charles or Cyril or Clayborn will come along and sweep you off your feet. Cheer up, May, it must mean something."

Yes, it must mean something.

"Did I tell you about old Mrs Chapman at number fifty?" she'd continue, cutting into another apple. "Poor old thing's been taken ill. Mrs Forest says it's, well, you know..."

Inevitably Mum would make a sorry face – perfectly genuine – and shake her head.

"No, what did Mrs Forest say?"

And Mother would have to prepare herself before saying it.

"Cancer." Immediately followed by spitting out three times across her left shoulder, three hurried darts of her tongue between her lips. "Spit out, May, quick, three times, come on."

And I'd have to do the same as if the action alone would save us both from the very same fate; I didn't question why, it was just something we did.

And it must mean something.

"Remember," Mum would constantly remind me, "when you or anyone else speaks of illness or death and someone sneezes on it, pull your left ear lobe three times. Don't hesitate, do it immediately. We don't want anything bad coming of it."

For some reason, that one always worried me the most.

I often stare at my reflection, wondering what new similarity has cropped up without me knowing, what little expression of Mother's has now become my own. I already have so many habits of hers. As for the superstitions, they're a part of me and more than I could ever have known back then, at the silly, arrogant age of seventeen when I tried to shrug it all off as meaningless. But, as Mother always said, "Everything happens for a reason."

Everything happens for a reason.

Saturday, 10th June, 1940

Aunt Celia has been nagging at me again and I've only been here four days. She thinks I should join the local troop of girl guides or whatever they're called. She says it'll, 'take me out of myself,' and that, 'helping others is our Christian gift.' I'm tired of hearing about Christian morals and being good, doing good, seeing the good in other people, except the Germans of course, they're all devil worshippers according to her and she can't see anything good in any single one of them. But she doesn't seem to care that I've lost my family in one go, and the only thing I have left of them is Mum's old tortoiseshell pen I'm writing with. And I might not have had even that if I hadn't pinched it from her dressing table the day I met Albert. I may as well talk to the pen, I can't talk to Aunt about anything; she won't let me speak if I mention anything about them, she just changes the subject and flatly refuses to respond. Maybe she thinks it's for the best – for myself or herself I can't tell – but either way, it's hard. I want to talk about them. I hear their voices in my head and I laugh at June's laughter; if I'm allowed to talk about them, I might be able to accept it but at the moment all I feel is a rage that I can't let out. I have to keep it all in. Nobody wants to see someone break down and scream at the sky or beat the ground with their fists and cry with anger because it's not the done thing. But that's what I want to do! "What will people think?" is all Aunt Celia would say.

I can't stand this pretence. I want to shout at the world, I want everyone to know how much pain I have inside me, I want to kick and scream out at God, "This isn't fair, why do you do this to us?" And I don't even believe in God. If only someone would let me get this anger out... but nobody wants to help, they'd rather ignore these emotions; stiff upper lip, get on with it, life must go on, it's no use sobbing, one must pick oneself up.

Mother was right, this English prudishness is absurd, why shouldn't we all show how we feel? If you're frowned upon for crying at the death of your family, then when is it acceptable to cry?

I hate it here. I wish I'd been at home when the factory exploded.

TWO

"May?"

"Yes, Aunt Celia?"

"Have you thought anymore about helping out for this weekend's fete at the hall? Miss Parker asked me only yesterday to remind you. We both think it would be a good idea for you to muck in, get to know people. She says she could do with an extra hand with the tea and cakes as the Leadbetter girl is helping serve out the front this year."

I didn't look up from my boiled egg. Instead, I stared at my soldiers and pondered whether I wanted them to be British or German.

"Are you listening to me, May?"

I think both, and I picked up two pieces of bread, putting them in my mouth at the same time.

Aunt Celia tutted and, from the corner of my eye, I saw her remove her glasses.

"Now," she started, "I've taken you into my home as any good Christian should, but I would please ask for a little civility in return. It's not much to ask of a niece, is it, to show her aunt respect and cordiality? I mean, it isn't as though you're the only one in the world suffering, or who has lost someone very dear to them. I lost both my own brother and a beautiful niece, remember, but you don't see me flaking out or crying over it. It's been over six weeks since the tragedy and you've hardly acquainted yourself with anybody. No, you must make the effort instead of moping about the village; people have already begun to talk, several times I've had to quell gossip that you're a bit, well, a bit of a funny girl. You never speak to anyone, you barely look them in the eye, always with your head down and eyes glued to the floor. It isn't natural for a young girl to behave in such a queer way. You should be making friends, you should have at least made one friend by now, you've been here over a month. What about that red-faced girl, Marjorie Wilson? She seems pleasant enough."

I swallowed the soldiers with difficulty and looked at my aunt through narrowed eyes; I felt like throwing my cup and saucer to the floor but, instead, I said, "She's only fourteen. What do I have in common with a fourteen-year-old? And besides, she smells like the cows in her father's barn."

"May! What a thing to say of another girl, you ought to be ashamed."

"But she does. It can't be helped, I suppose, living with a herd of cattle… but it doesn't mean I want to be around *her*."

I could see how shocked my aunt was by my honesty.

Mum, you were right again.

Aunt Celia began cleaning her glasses with the edge of the tablecloth. Her eyebrows were raised as high as they could reach, and her pink lips pinched in tightly.

After a minute of silence, she put the spectacles back on her nose and turned to me.

"Listen to me. You will go and help out at the fete this weekend and there will be nothing more said on the subject."

And that was that. We finished our breakfast in silence, apart from the constant tick-tocking from the clock on the mantelpiece and the bark of a dog down the lane. Someone shouted and the dog quietened down.

Poor thing, I know how you feel.

I brushed crumbs from my hands onto my empty plate and then got up from the table.

"Are you all done, Aunt?" I asked politely.

"Yes, thank you, May. What do you intend to do now, then?"

"I had thought about going for a walk."

"Well, in that case you can take this letter round to the Leadbetters at Ivy Cottage."

I don't want to see anyone, I don't want to have to make silly small talk.

"Very well, Aunt," I said, a little too flushed with annoyance.

She gave me a long hard stare.

"Thank you, May. And when you've done that, you must come back and check if I have any other errands for you to run, I know I shall need a hand packing some odds and ends for the swap table next week. We all help each other in Guilsbridge."

I took the letter from her outstretched hand and tucked it into my skirt pocket before piling the breakfast things onto the tray.

"And another thing," my aunt went on, "it's about time you thought about doing some real work, find yourself a job to help with the war effort. We all must do our bit."

I nodded but said nothing.

I'd only taken a couple of steps into the hall when I heard my aunt sigh and say, "If only it had been baby June, at least I would've had a charge whom I could teach. Too much like her mother, regrettably."

I smiled and kicked open the kitchen door.

On the first day I arrived, I'd discovered a footpath through the fields which led me alongside old barns and high hedgerows, and I would walk as often as I could. I liked being alone. I liked to be able to think without anyone interrupting with pointless nonsense. For a long time, I would think of home and my parents and sister, but today I had something else to think about.

"Lizzie Leadbetter," I said between gritted teeth, and swatting at the air with a yellow stem of grass. Everything had started turning yellow. The summer sun showed no sign of yielding to clouds and everyone bemoaned the fact that rain hadn't fallen for over two weeks. People were agitated. The crops would die. The animals would die.

"And what about the fete?" they cried!

"Stupid fete," I said, now chewing on the end of the grass stem and looking across the fields. "Stupid villagers, don't they know they've killed and eaten most of the animals, anyway." And I suddenly remembered the dog barking earlier that morning followed by the quietness.

"Better not have," I shouted, feeling sick and angry, "or I'll, I'll... I'll put a curse on them!"

I knew I couldn't curse anybody – Mum had warned me against thoughts of those kind – but it didn't stop me wanting to. The way I had started feeling towards others scared and excited me.

I reached an old farm gate and swung myself up, sitting with one leg either side. The sun blazed down. Bright light –

so bright it made your eyes water – seemed to illuminate the world, making all the terrifying things more real.

I'd never known heat like it.

I sighed and spat out my grass stem which fell point first, lodging amongst its kin, sideways. I continued to stare at it, feeling the back of my neck burn.

"Let it burn."

And then I remembered Lizzie Leadbetter.

I'd taken Aunt Celia's letter to the Leadbetters, as she'd asked, but had the misfortune to come face to face with Lizzie, a girl of my age but with a rather spoilt and arrogant air about her. She'd opened the door as I was about to poke the letter through the letterbox. I really didn't like her, although she was very good at showing people what she wanted them to see, but not the truth of herself. And I think she realised that I saw straight through it.

"What are you doing?" she'd said, looking down her nose at me. It took all my strength of will not to slap her across the face, but I'd managed to answer that my aunt had a letter for Mrs Leadbetter.

"I see," she'd replied from up high, snatching it from my hand, and I'd turned to walk away when she called, "Oh, wait a moment, will you?"

I should've ignored her, why didn't I just ignore her? Mother always told me about girls like her, how they're not to be trusted because vanity and the self are more important to them than anything else. She would have had a few choice words to say about Lizzie Leadbetter, and she would've made me roar with laughter with her insults.

But, in that moment, I wished I'd had a shot gun, and I know Mother would've approved if I'd blasted the stupid, vain cow to Kingdom Come.

"You're the orphan, aren't you?" she'd said.

I was dumbstruck.

"Lost both parents and a sister, wasn't it? Shame. Lucky for me I still have both parents, and my grandmother. It must be awful to be you."

I'd not been able to do a thing, except stare at her in shock.

"My father's away, he's a fighter pilot, everyone says how brave he is. Did your father join up? Oh, no, that's right isn't it, he had something wrong with him, didn't he? That's what I've heard anyway. And that's how he came to be caught up in the explosion, I suppose, with his feet up at home. Shame."

You bitch, I kept thinking, my body shaking. *You horrible, spiteful bitch. I'll get you, I'll get you back for that, just you wait.*

I don't know how long we had both stood there, but it felt like forever, and the hatred welled up inside me as I glared at her. I felt it in my gaze, the absolute venom pouring out of me, and it must've shown as Lizzie gave off signs of discomfort. If it hadn't been for her old grandmother calling for her, I think she may've had a tantrum. She'd seemed to come to her senses at that point, and after giving me another unkind smile, she shut the door in my face.

As I reflected on all that had happened, I became agitated in my impotence. I wanted to get her back, there and then, I wanted to run to her house and push her to the ground, I wanted to pull her hair out and scratch her eyes out and kick her until I no longer had any strength left.

But I knew I couldn't do any of that.

How can I get her back? What can I do?

I looked up and saw the shimmering fields of white barley; there were men and women in the far distance, working away, and I knew it'd only be a matter of time before Aunt Celia suggested again that I 'do my bit'. I didn't want to.

I didn't want to do anything but run and hide from everyone and be left alone.

"What can I *do*?" I muttered again, my thoughts returning to Lizzie, "She isn't going to get away with it, I shan't let her."

I wiped my forehead with the sleeve of my white blouse, fully knowing I had a handkerchief in my pocket which my aunt had impressed on me.

"Help me, Mum," I said, looking to the blue sky, and I squinted, my eyes watering, "you'd have told me how to repay that unkindness. *She* started it and you always said that it was fair game after that."

I hung my head. My grass stem had slipped further into the rest and I swiped at it with my foot. I couldn't quite reach and I got angry very quickly; I started kicking at the grass, just kicking and kicking, until I had to jump from the gate in order to kick out harder.

"Lizzie bloody Leadbetter. I hate you, I hate you!" and I began kicking the gate, holding on tightly to the top bar. The sweat poured from me and I didn't care; I kept on kicking, thinking it was Lizzie Leadbetter, and I started to cry.

"Hey! What the hell do you think you're doing?"

I looked up; Mr Gumby, with his ferret and sack, stood fifty yards from me. Even from that distance I could see how deranged he thought I was.

I wiped my face and then gestured a wave.

Mr Gumby was the man to go to if you wanted rabbit.

"I said 'what do you think you're doing?'" he asked again, walking towards me.

I straightened my hair and adjusted my blouse, trying to appear as ladylike as I could muster, knowing full well he'd go and tell Aunt all about my strange behaviour.

"Well? What have you got to say for yourself?" he said, towering over me. I raised my eyes level with his chest and saw his ferret poking out from under his lightweight jacket. Its bright black eyes looked back at me, pale pink nose twitching constantly, making his whiskers jump up and down.

I smiled at him and started to cry again.

"Eh, what's all this, young lady?" Mr Gumby asked, and he put down his sack and took me by the shoulders.

"Don't tell Aunt Celia, please!" I sobbed, feeling like an idiot, "I just feel so angry and it's only an old gate, I didn't think anyone would care!"

"Now, now, stop this crying. No one's hurt you, have they? Come on, sit down and take a breath. You'll sob your eyes inside out if you carry on like this."

He sat me down on the middle bar of the gate and I gradually came to my senses.

"I'm sorry, Mr Gumby," I said quietly, and not looking at his face, "I miss my family."

"Of course you do, my dear, it'd be a heartless person who didn't."

We both were quiet for a moment.

"It's an unfair world, missy," he carried on, "but we're here and that's all there is to it. I was wrong to shout at you, but I thought you were a little vandal, I couldn't see your tears. I should've left you to it. Get it out, get all that anger out, there's no harm in knocking bells out of this old gate, after all."

I wiped my face with the back of my hand and gave a small smile.

"I'll tell you this, though," he went on, lifting me up by the elbow, "I shall keep it to myself that you don't use a handkerchief like a proper young lady ought."

"Thank you," I said, with a sigh. "My aunt wouldn't be very happy at all if she knew. And I'm tired of being nagged."

"Well," Mr Gumby said, picking up his sack and throwing it over his shoulder, "perhaps you'd better start thinking of helping your aunt a bit more. There's nothing wrong with working to help keep other folk off your back." From inside his jacket, the ferret turned to look up at his master. "Isn't that right, lad?" and Mr Gumby rubbed the ferret's head with a thick index finger.

"What's his name?" I asked, fascinated by the strange animal.

"Just lad, we don't give working animals names, makes it harder to…" but he stopped abruptly, "…anyway, I'd better get along. Now you take care, young miss, and mind you don't break anything with that anger of yours… like your big toe for instance."

I watched him wander away across the fields.

"I suppose he's right," and I shrugged.

I leaned against the gate, thinking, but I couldn't fix my mind on one thing. The summer, the war, the heat, the fete, Mr Gumby's ferret, Lizzie Leadbetter, Aunt Celia, the villagers, the picture of Pageant Road after the explosion, the barking dog down the lane, Mum, Dad and June…

I shook my head.

"No," I said quietly and knitting my brow. "He's only right about one thing. The world isn't fair, not when people like her don't suffer but people like me do. She's got everything I want! And she doesn't deserve it."

I fixed my mind's eye on her face and felt my mouth tighten.

"You don't deserve anything."

Sunday morning, 22ⁿᵈ July

Another air raid last night, must've been about one o'clock when I heard them coming. Such an eerie sound, terrifying really, not simply because of what they're bringing but the sound itself. I doubt I'll ever get used to it. Aunt Celia and I hurried to the The King's Head as all villagers are meant to, those without a shelter anyway. We spent a few hours in the cellar, a few told stories to while away the time or quieten down the little ones, but I had brought my book along and closed myself off from the rest.

When we eventually emerged, the birds were in full song and everything carried on as normal. I suppose the raid has spurred everyone on to get the fete going as soon as possible and enjoy themselves.

Aunt Celia looked worried. She said something about London being wiped off the face of the Earth, I could see how upset she was, but I did nothing to comfort her. She wouldn't want it anyway. I doubt she'd cope with any form of affection from me.

And so I've decided, I know exactly what I'm going to do to pay back that Lizzie, and it's all thanks to a conversation I overheard yesterday between Miss Parker and that awful girl. They were outside Miss Parker's as I was on my way back from my walk – which Aunt Celia detests me doing – and I heard mention of Miss Elizabeth's favourite type of bun. Miss Parker gave a squeal which, I suppose, meant delight as she herself had made those very buns and would put one by for her at the fete. The usual sickening responses from the spoilt cow.

It may not be the coldest dish served and, given the greater scheme of things, have any importance at all, but it will certainly make me feel better and that's what I need right now, something for me. Aunt Celia will never forgive me. She may even ask me to leave; there's been mention of her taking in an evacuee from London and if she resents my being here already, then who knows what she'll do when her precious reputation is tarnished once more for having me as a relative.

Mother would love it. She would also have laughed her head off if she knew how irritated Aunt Celia became when I insisted on playing chop sticks on her piano in the 'parlour'. I could hear her shouting from the kitchen, but I just plonked down harder. It even got on my nerves, but it was worth it. I don't know why I must anger Aunt so. Maybe I do, maybe it's because I know she disliked my mum. And anyone who dislikes my mum is an enemy.

I must get dressed and have breakfast. Church service at nine o'clock – yawn – and after that, all the fun and games of the fete.

Three

She came in wearing a yellow gingham dress, her hair had been washed and put up in a ponytail which she swished around whenever she walked to and from tables. She chatted and giggled and pranced about, always swishing the pony tail.

I stood behind the tea urn, my arms folded across my chest, and watched her display.

"You wait," I muttered, glaring at her, "you and your stupid ponytail." And then I smiled.

It had been easier than I expected; Miss Parker wanted me to serve the cakes and buns and pour the tea while she washed and dried the crockery.

At about half past two, Miss Parker came out from the tiny kitchen, a big smile on her face.

"May," she said, in trembling sort of voice. She was a spinster with long grey hair forever tied up in a top-knot, and she clasped her thin, red hands together, high up to her chest. I didn't really mind Miss Parker, she seemed quiet and thoughtful, someone I could appreciate. "When you have a break, do try one of those lovely iced-buns, old Mrs Cartwell made them fresh this morning. Have a treat, I'm grateful to you for helping."

I thanked her, and she patted my arm before turning back to the kitchen when she suddenly stopped and swung round.

"Oh, I very nearly forgot. It's time for Lizzie to have a sit down, the poor girl's been on her feet since midday. Lizzie! Lizzie! Come and have a cup of tea and that Glory bun you chose earlier."

I couldn't help grinning.

"Coming, Miss Parker," Lizzie called. She was crouched down next to a couple of elderly gentlemen I didn't know, and they were chuckling at something she said. She stood up and whispered something to one of the men who then grasped her hand and shook it warmly.

I hated her even more and was beginning to wish I'd thought of another way to get her back. My silly plan now seemed incredibly childish and simple.

"Too late now," I muttered, watching her move between the tables, her head up high. She passed by me with a nod, one which told me I was beneath her, and sauntered into the kitchen. She soon returned with a plate.

"So," she said, looking me up and down, and I clenched my fists, "you decided to help after all. Normally *I* do your job, but they thought I'd be much better 'out front,' as it were. They say I have a way with people, charm, you know?"

She held back a laugh.

"Hmm," she went on, "perhaps you *don't* know."

And she walked away, giggling.

Oh, how I hated her!

She sat herself down with a couple called Mason. I watched intently. Someone asked me for tea, but I barely heard.

"I think I shall have a drop of tea, please."

"Sorry, what?"

"A cup of tea, please, if it's not too much trouble. And we don't say, 'what', we say, 'I beg your pardon'. Really, May, whatever did your mother teach you?"

It was my aunt.

"Oh, yes, of course, Aunt Celia, and I *do* beg your pardon."

I hurriedly poured the tea, hardly looking at what I was doing, when I heard such a squeal it sounded like a trapped piglet.

Everyone turned to see Lizzie Leadbetter, her hands over her mouth, and stamping on the floor with her tanned-leather shoes.

"Whatever's the matter?" the Masons asked, but she couldn't speak.

I glanced over at her plate and saw that she'd eaten half of the Glory bun. I couldn't help but chuckle.

"What are you giggling at, May?" my aunt asked, rather severely.

I didn't answer but hid my smile with my hand.

Lizzie squealed again and pointed to her plate; the Masons peered at it, Mrs Mason pulled the plate closer to herself before flinging it back.

"How revolting! Whoever would do such a thing?"

"What's happened?" Aunt Celia asked, stepping over to their table.

"Someone's tampered with Lizzie's bun, look."

It didn't take a second for Aunt to realise who the culprit was. She turned to me, glaring, and I let my arm fall to my side. I gazed back at her and shrugged. She walked towards me and leaned in close to my face.

"Young lady, if that despicable trick has anything to do with you, I shall be very angry."

I said nothing.

"May... I think it would be wise if you were to leave right now. I'll explain to Miss Parker that you're feeling unwell, but I shall be having serious words with you when I come home." She gave a sharp nod before striding behind the counter to find Miss Parker.

I didn't feel anything. I watched the vain girl sobbing, I watched the Masons comfort her and spoil her with sympathetic crooning and I watched the rest of the villagers turn to stare at me.

"She did it! She's always so mean to me!" and Lizzie Leadbetter pointed her finger at me, "it was her!"

I gazed at all the disapproving faces; they seemed expectant of an explanation or apology but, instead, I began untying my apron. I pulled the cloth away from me, threw it on the counter and walked out from behind the tea urn. That's when the muttering and whispering started.

"Shameful girl, she should never have come."

"It's her aunt I feel sorry for, poor Mrs Sanders."

"What kind of a mother did she have? She shouldn't have been allowed to have children if that's the way she brought them up."

I stopped in my tracks and turned to face Mrs Mason. I must've had a face like thunder for she suddenly shrank into her seat, her eyebrows raised in alarm.

"What did you say?" I asked quietly. I glared at her and Mr Mason coughed.

"Never mind what she said, girl, I think it's time you were on your way."

"What did she say about my mother?" I asked, barely moving my lips, my teeth clenched.

Everyone was silent.

"Tell me what she said."

"How dare you speak to your elders like that!" Mrs Mason suddenly blurted out, her face red.

I felt rage in my chest. I started to shake. I was about to erupt when I heard Aunt Celia cry, "May! Home at once!"

I flashed a look at her; she stood with her handbag in the crook of her arm, her white gloves so bright in the dingy village hall, and her shocked face ashen with embarrassment.

I looked back at the Masons and Lizzie, who now had a small grin on her face, and cursed them silently.

And then I left. I strode out of the hall and into the sunshine, where games were being played and shrieking children ran about with paper cones of home-made sweets.

I walked past Mr Pritchard and his sow, fenced in with a bale of straw as a few people tried to guess her weight. She grunted, breathing heavily and I looked at her, her big wet snout resting on the low plank.

I strode past a game of Aunt Sally, children and adults alike all throwing wooden balls at her head, nobody following any of the rules. They seemed so intent on hurting her, a pack of wild villagers desperate to cause as much damage as possible.

I sneered at them as I went by, pretending I didn't care and that my confidence overrode everything. But I knew I wanted to cry.

My pace quickened. I heard the high-pitched voices of the happy children and felt the heat pounding through me.

I untied my red ribbon from my hair as I started to run, the jeering laughter of the men and women playing games spurred me on, away from them, and I felt my hair stream behind me in the wind.

I let go of my red ribbon as I reached the edge of the green and ran into the empty road, turning down Cherry Hill Lane.

The village, so quiet, for once appeared beautiful to me and as I ran past cottages, I saw all the roses and hollyhocks, all the bright colours of living things and their green leaves. I could smell the wisteria that smothered end walls and porchways and then, the scent of lavender growing like grey hedges along the front of Miss Parker's garden. Bees droned amongst the bright purple heads and red admirals dropped and drifted into the ivy that spread along the stone wall.

I felt my breath catch in my throat and I burst into tears.

"Mother!"

The tears gathered and poured down my face. On I ran, heading for Long Lane and to the fields that I knew would be empty.

When I reached the stile, I collapsed onto the wooden plank and held onto the post, crying harder and harder until my head ached.

I tried to scream out my pain, but words couldn't be formed, and I sobbed and raged until I no longer had the energy to cry.

When at last I became calm, I found myself gazing at the wooden post, seeing beyond it and seeing nothing.

I took shallow breaths, worn out with emotion, and could only mutter one thing: "I wish I was dead."

Suddenly I sneezed.

I raised my hand to my ear, ready to pull on the lobe three times, but I stopped myself. I looked up to the blue sky.

I won't, not this time.

I waited, breathing more rapidly, and allowed my arm to fall back to my side.

Shouldn't I, though? Mother would never…

"But she's dead!" I suddenly shouted, standing up on the stile, "she's gone! They've all gone! What good were those stupid superstitions to her if she's dead anyway! They didn't save her! Pulling ear lobes, spitting out three times, what's the use in that?"

I wiped my face, roughly.

"Spitting out three times didn't stop the factory exploding, did it? Or not picking up a pair of scissors she'd dropped, if she had would that mean the explosion would've been worse? Killed her twice? No! I hate those stupid things she taught me, I hate them."

I hung my head in grief.

"She's dead," I whispered, "and nothing will bring her back. Not salt over my shoulder or keeping heather in my bag, nothing."

My sore and swollen eyes scanned the fields and hedgerows. I had calmed down and now breathed with a sense of relief.

"I'm sorry, Mother, I'm so sorry."

I wiped the back of my hand across my mouth and rubbed my eyes, trying to blink away the puffiness and wishing for a nearby stream so that I could bathe my hot face.

I jumped down onto the grass and took a deep breath.

When I glanced up, a shadow had appeared on the horizon.

"Oh no," I whispered, "who's that?"

It had to be a villager, the angle of the sun made it impossible for this to be the young oak tree growing in the hedgerow behind – but I couldn't make anything out.

A sudden shiver ran through me and I rubbed my arms to rid me of goosebumps. The afternoon sky began to change; beyond the oak and the figure, grey clouds formed, and the atmosphere felt different.

I watched as the silver-edged clouds deepened, until the wind blew and the sky above the far field turned darker.

When I looked to the villager, he appeared bigger, fuller. I strained to see again and this time it looked as though he carried something on his back.

"Who *is* that?"

A thread of light cracked across the darkening clouds and I felt exposed. I scanned the bright blue sky above me and then felt the cool wind on my face.

Another trail of lightning split the blackening clouds.

I didn't want to go back to the village and yet I didn't want to stay; the countryside suddenly worried me. I was alone, far from anyone, but another flash of lightning made my mind up for me.

"*She'll* be waiting, I suppose," I muttered, turning back to the stranger, my hair flicking about my face in the hardening wind.

"What's that, now?"

He had one arm held up high and, as I squinted, there came a flash of light in a mirror. My heart leapt and I gasped for air.

"What the heck happened there?" I said, clinging onto the post.

With an uneasy sense of oppression, and without looking behind, I hurried home.

Sunday, 22nd July, evening

I only just got home in time before the heavens opened. I heard the villagers screaming and then watched from the front room window as they rushed about in the downpour. I don't think anyone expected a storm; it seemed to come out of nowhere.

Aunt was waiting in the parlour. She was sitting in the armchair with that annoying clock ticking away. It drives me mad.

She had her say – nothing new to tell – except now she thinks that I'm a destructive influence and thanks God I haven't made any friends, especially Marjorie Wilson, as I'm likely to corrupt her. As if I ever would, I don't have anything against Marjorie, she's just a girl who smells of cow pats.

After apologising a hundred times for my actions (she saw straight through my lie that I knew nothing about the bun incident and, really, I failed to care whether she knew the truth or not), I explained to her why I felt the need to do it in the first place. She did listen. But she didn't believe that a girl such as Lizzie Leadbetter could be so cruel and say such nasty things.

"But she did," I told her, "I wouldn't have wanted to pay her back otherwise, because there'd be nothing to pay her back for."

Aunt sighed at that point and then said the most ridiculous thing.

"That's how wars start."

"Is that how this one started?" I cried. "Did Hitler say something insulting about Chamberlain's mother?"

She then told me to go to my room and only come down when supper's ready and so here I am, writing at my dressing table, looking out onto the lane with all its trees in full leaf and with the rain pattering down. It's so gloomy, you wouldn't think it to be only half past six. And I can hear that clock, even from up here. How does she ever put up with it? One day, I might just accidentally smash the thing; it makes me nervous, tick-tock, tick-tock, on and on. I can feel my heart try and beat in time with it. Stupid.

Oh, there we go, Aunt has called that tea is ready. Or rather, 'supper', I'm not allowed to call it tea anymore. Apparently, tea is what you have in the afternoons.

I may write more later, it all depends on what thrilling events occur between now and then.

Four

The small, round table in the parlour had been set with a lace cloth and teapot, teacups and saucers. There were plates of sardines, sliced boiled eggs, bread and cold meat which, I assumed, was rabbit. I didn't like eating rabbit, the colour of it put me off, but food was food.

The two lamps were on and the strange early darkness from outside seemed to want to get inside and partake of some of the cosiness; I had to admit, it did look lovely with the warmth of the orange lights, and I found myself simply looking all around at Aunt's things and how beautiful it all appeared. The piano especially. Aunt had placed a vase of roses in the centre and I gathered by the way the surface gleamed and shone, that she had polished it, you could see everything reflected, as though another room lay inside the piano itself.

Aunt Celia drew the blackouts.

I sat down and lay a napkin across my lap. Aunt Celia nodded in approval.

"Excellent, May, you seem to be learning," she said, pulling her chair from under the table.

I felt too tired to bite and instead replied, "Yes, Aunt, I feel as though I've learnt a lot today."

This pleased my aunt very much and, I suppose, it pleased her most of all because she assumed the credit.

"I am very glad to hear it. Once you apologise to the Leadbetter girl tomorrow, we can all start afresh," and she sat down.

I bit my lip hard. I would never apologise to that girl, but I thought it wise not to say so at that moment.

Aunt Celia laid a tea strainer over my cup and began pouring the tea in silence. I watched the wet leaves gather in the strainer and I suddenly felt overwhelmed with sadness.

"Aunt," I asked, "can I please not have the leaves strained?"

She looked at me as if I had asked the most absurd thing she'd ever heard.

"Whatever for?"

"I, err… I just want to…" I tailed off and found myself twisting the napkin round and round with my fingers.

"Whatever is the matter?" Aunt Celia asked, placing the teapot down, "I hope you're not thinking of those peculiar habits of your mother's? I shall be very cross if you are. I've told you, this is a Christian household and I shall stand for none of that heathen nonsense."

She shook her head and tutted before placing the strainer over her own cup and pouring the tea.

"Now then," she went on, ignoring everything, "what would you like? A little sardine?"

I nodded. She poked a small fish with a fork and dropped it onto my plate.

"Bread?"

"Yes, please, Aunt."

A slice of brown bread was delicately placed onto my side plate.

"Oh, dear," my aunt exclaimed, and, standing up, "I forgot to bring in the cake Miss Parker gave us. We're lucky she gave us anything after your behaviour today," and she swept out of the parlour and into the passage.

I quickly threw my tea back into the pot before hurriedly stirring up the leaves. I then poured out some more without using the strainer.

"Here we are then," Aunt said, on her return, "it's only a small portion of carrot cake but it's better than nothing," and she majestically placed it in the middle of the table, like some sort of centre piece to be proud of.

"It was very kind of Miss Parker," I muttered, taking a small bite out of my slice of bread. I chewed slowly.

"Yes, indeed. Now, back to the point. Tomorrow you shall apologise to Elizabeth and then see if help is needed packing away the things from the fete."

She took a sip of tea, her little finger raised high. I looked at her face; she had her eyebrows raised and her eyelids stretched, revealing a line of make-up clogged in a deep crease of skin.

Who do you think you are?

I dropped my bread on my plate and took a sip of my own tea. Tiny flecks of leaves drifted on the surface.

Sunday teatime, you reading the leaves to Dad, him nodding but not understanding... you winking at me when he wasn't looking. I'll read them upstairs, Aunt will never know, I'll read them for you, tonight...

Silence claimed the parlour. But for the clock there were no other sounds, and we both ate our suppers without speaking a word. The wind had died away and no more rain fell against the windows.

I looked around at the vase of pink roses smelling of summer, and the warm glow of the room made their heads glow like peaches.

Peaches... I remember having one fresh. Dad had bought one for each of us...

Suddenly, the heads of the roses shed all their petals at once. I half-saw them collapse onto the piano top as I remembered the taste of that strange, sweet fruit.

I frowned, staring at the mass of rose petals. The lamps flickered with a crackle. I heard Aunt tutting and muttering and I glanced up, wondering why she moaned.

"These lights," she muttered, "I would much rather have gas."

I was about to disagree when something caught my eye; beyond the vase, in the corner of the room, a long shadow had appeared. It spread up, along the join.

That looks like a person.

I could see the roundness of shoulders and the shape of the head. The continued flickering light distorted what I imagined but, at moments, the shoulders appeared bulkier and the head seemed to flash up pictures of bull horns.

"Bother it," my aunt said, getting up from the table and flinging her napkin onto her empty plate. She strode over to one of the lamps and switched it off. "May, fetch some candles from the top drawer, would you? I cannot bear flickering electric light, it makes me nervous."

I shook my head, bringing myself back to the evening, and stood up.

"Whatever caused all those roses to shed their petals like that?" I asked, handing two candles to Aunt Celia.

She hadn't appeared to notice. After fixing the candles in their holders and lighting them, she turned her attention to the flowers.

"Dear me, what a mess. They were fresh today. I picked them myself from the garden, what a nuisance. May, if you've finished, clear the table while I tidy this up – the nectar leaves sticky marks – and I've only just polished the piano this morning."

She tutted again, switching off the remaining lamp.

I turned to face the crockery and remnants of food. I'd hardly eaten anything but I didn't feel hungry, all I wanted was tea and so I carried everything to the kitchen apart from my teacup, teapot and the small jug of milk.

After clearing the supper things away, I settled back in my chair at the table.

"Would you like another cup of tea, Aunt?"

"No, thank you, May, I'm just wondering…" and she fell silent. She held a handful of petals and was looking at them hard, "Yes, I think I shall just pop next door and see if Mr Roberts has any idea about this. I can't see any brown spots or black fly but if the roses *are* diseased then I must nip it in the bud. They all looked so fresh and healthy this afternoon but now…"

I sipped my tea.

"He'll know what's wrong, I'm sure. He has such a way with plants," and she went into the passage. I heard her pull on her raincoat and imagined her plumping up her hair in the mirror above the telephone seat. "I shan't be long!" she called, and the front door slammed shut behind her.

I sighed with relief; if Mr Roberts had his way, visitors would be held to ransom all night long as he waxed lyrical about his precious flowers and just how much he knew about horticulture.

I liked being alone in the house, I could feel how it would be to live there in peace, and I especially liked it as now I could do the leaves without hiding it from Aunt.

I drained my tea, careful with the last few sips; you had to get as much of the liquid out without getting a mouthful of leaves, before casting three circles with the cup – left to right – and then quickly turn it upside down onto the saucer.

I waited for a minute, letting any excess tea drain away. It had always been frustrating to peer into your teacup, full of interesting shapes and letters, only for drops of liquid to run and ruin whatever images there had been.

As I waited, I became transfixed by that same corner of the room.

Tick-tock. Tick-tock.

"It looks like the shadow of someone real."

Tick-tock.

"Strange day," I said, trying to keep my heart from racing. I breathed deeply and suddenly thought, *What if this has got something to do with earlier?*

I lay my hands on the tablecloth and gazed down at my up-turned teacup for a few minutes, thinking about the possibility of Mum being right all along.

"Don't be so stupid," and I snatched up my cup.

The leaves had all gathered near the 'house'. A long figure with something across its shoulders.

I concentrated.

"Who could that be?"

His legs stretched to the rim of the cup and would've continued for I couldn't see his feet. But the legs were thin and they bowed near the top.

"Could be… Mr Gumby? With his sack across his back?"

I chewed my lower lip.

"No, I'm sure Mr Gumby doesn't have such thin legs."

The body was thick with tea leaves, very dark and dense so that it bulged towards me, and the arms reached up, as if holding onto whatever lay over his shoulders.

"It could be that man I saw in the field. If it is, Mum would say he's trying to tell me something."

I held the cup up and turned it in the light.

"I can't see… what's that?"

The shoulders were wide but the head appeared distorted because of the shape of the tea cup; it lay flat at the base and was rather faint compared to the rest of him.

"Looks like…"

I squinted.

"No," I whispered, "can't be… it looks like bull horns."

I glanced to the corner of the room, but the shadow had gone.

I sat and thought for a moment of the coincidences playing out, and the ticking of the clock disturbed me as I wondered more and more about the man in the field. I remembered the flash of light – I saw it in my mind's eye – and my heart leapt again.

Something cold seeped along my hand and I looked down.

The entire image in tea leaves had crept over the edge of the cup and now spread along the length of my thumb. I watched, fascinated, until I yelled out and threw the cup on the table. It fell off the edge and smashed as I desperately wiped the leaves from my hand and flung them to the floor, whimpering as I did so.

"What the…? What's going on?"

The figure appeared to have grown feet but not those of a human. They looked like the feet of a bird.

I quickly stood up, knocking my chair backwards, and pulled at my hair, scraping my fingers across my scalp.

This is too strange, this isn't just coincidence… what was that? How did it do that?

And, for the first time, I wished for my Aunt Celia.

I stood for some moments, biting my nails and shaking at what had happened until it suddenly dawned on me.

"For goodness sake, you didn't let it drain properly, that's all," and I tutted at myself before stepping over to the broken cup on the floor. "She is *not* going to be pleased when she finds out," and I carefully picked up the pieces, placing them on the table. I then fetched some old newspapers and began wrapping up the broken crockery.

But I couldn't help but think of the shadow and the tea leaves and that strange figure in the field.

"They all looked the same," I whispered, rolling the paper up tight.

Suddenly, the front door slammed.

"Hello, May, I'm back," and Aunt Celia swept into the room. She had a smile on her face, but it dropped when she saw me at the table. "Whatever has happened?"

"I had an accident with the tea cup. I'm sorry, Aunt, but I dropped it and it smashed."

She closed her eyes. I saw her nostrils flare as she slowly shook her head, and I slumped.

"I am sorry, Aunt Celia."

"Never mind," she said, but in a tone that implied she did.

I took a step back as she approached and hung my head, waiting for her next question.

"But," she began, looking down at the rug, "what on Earth is all of this?" She bent down and wiped a finger over the floor before bringing it close to her face. "Are these tea leaves?"

"Yes, Aunt."

"Look at me, May."

I raised my head slightly.

"Have you been," she stopped and gave a sharp sigh, "have you been reading tea leaves in my house? What have I said about your mother's ridiculous superstitions and fancies? I will not have any sorcery or black magic happen under this roof, is that clear?"

"It's hardly sorcery, Aunt, I only did it to feel close to Mum again."

"Really? I hardly see that as an excuse to perform witchcraft in a Christian household. Whatever would the neighbours think?"

"It's only a bit of fun," I murmured. I turned my head and gazed at the piano, the bright gleaming piano that had another world inside, and I wished I could get in.

"Now go and get a cloth and clean up this mess, then you can go to your room. I've had quite enough of your antics today."

I nodded and left.

Sunday night, 22nd July

All in all, it's been a terrible day, and I had such high hopes this morning. If an air raid happened right now I think I should probably just sit here and see what came of it. On their way back to France, they'd probably dump whatever bombs they had left and hit everything else except this house.

Aunt is very cross with me but there's nothing unusual about that. And she wants me to say sorry to the spoilt cow tomorrow but I'm not going to. It'll only make things worse, not saying sorry, but I cannot – will not – bring myself to apologise to that hideous girl. It was funny, though, however brief. I'll never forget the way she squealed.

I don't know how to put this, but as I've got nobody in the world to talk to, I shall have to write it down. Something strange happened today, well, a couple of things really. I don't know if I'm imagining it or not, it could just be my mind playing tricks – it has been such a long, emotional week what with the raids and lack of sleep – and I do tell myself not to be so silly, but Mum hammered into me to expect the strange and inexplicable, and it's always there, lurking at the back of my mind. She would've taken each incident of today, linked them together and then looked at me with horror, I know she would.

Well, after running away from the fete, I saw someone in the field past Long Lane. He stood in the distance and I couldn't see him properly, not the detail. But then a storm came out of nowhere, and they seemed so connected, that lone figure and the sudden change in the weather. And I could've sworn I saw a flash of light in a mirror, but I can't be sure now. It could've been lightning I suppose. It has been exceptionally hot and muggy for weeks and a storm was inevitable to clear the air.

See, just writing it down and reading over it has helped. There's nothing sinister in someone I don't recognise standing in a field. And as for the shadow in the parlour, well, that's just me looking into things too deeply, seeing things that aren't there.

The same goes for the tea reading (yes, I did it. And yes, Aunt Celia found out. And yes, it's another black mark against me); it was just a mass of wet leaves clumped together in a big blob with bits coming off it. I've been trained to imagine, to make pictures out of stupid meaningless shapes and there we have it, I work myself up into a tizzy because of a meaningless blob in a tea cup.

Then again, I did sneeze when I wished I was dead, and I didn't pull my ear.

Just stop it, May, don't talk yourself into it again. You're tired, upset and alone. It's no wonder your brain is playing tricks.

Well, as there's nothing else to do, I suppose I should get into bed. It's only half past eight but I'm exhausted. I think I shall read a bit more of The Moon and Sixpence.

Write more tomorrow.

Five

I awoke, panicked, thinking I'd heard a Stuka passing overhead, and I sat bolt upright, listening hard.

There were no sounds, only the clock from the parlour.

I breathed a huge sigh of relief.

I hadn't really thought much about the war, not as much as I probably ought to have done. I felt too absorbed in my own world to bother with the outside and, living in rural Northamptonshire with no significant locations nearby to bomb, apart from the railway, I felt the war was happening somewhere else.

The only time I did realise was when the German planes flew over, and the sound of them terrified me.

"Must've been dreaming," I yawned, and snuggled back down under my top sheet.

I don't know how long I had been dozing but I'd reached the point of slipping back into a deep sleep when I heard a distant droning and I half-opened my eyes. I concentrated.

The heavy drone grew louder and I shot out of bed.

"They're coming!"

And I rushed from the bedroom and into my aunt's.

"Quick, we must get to the shelter, Aunt Celia! They're coming, hurry!"

Aunt Celia leapt from under her blanket and snatched her gown from the chair by her window.

"Quickly, May, run."

And we rushed downstairs, through the front door and into the lane.

Once outside, we both noticed how quiet the night was and we stood for a moment, looking up at the stars.

"May, there are no planes."

"But I heard them!"

"Well, all I can say is you must've been dreaming. Now let's get back inside before we wake the neighbours."

I shuffled back into the house.

"I'm sorry," I said, "false alarm. I'm sorry for waking you."

"Not to worry," my aunt said, in a kind tone which surprised me, "better to be safe than sorry. I would much rather be woken up and find out it's a false alarm than not to be woken up and be bombed in my bed."

It was the most human thing she'd ever said to me.

"Now, back upstairs with you."

We wished one another goodnight and returned to our bedrooms.

As I climbed back into bed, the old stead creaking, I pondered on the noise of the planes.

"It reminds of those hornets we had one summer, nesting in the roof of the shed," I whispered, looking up to the dark ceiling, "how loud they were, droning past me as they flew off for their food. And then Dad killed them all. I remember not liking him for a long while after that."

I lay quietly for a few minutes, thinking, before pulling the sheet over my face as the tick-tock of the parlour clock got inside my head.

"Please, just stop," I moaned, rolling over and clutching the sheet tighter over my ears. My face quickly became hot and I struggled to breathe. I ripped the sheet from me and lay with wide eyes, heart thumping, and felt my anger grow.

"Damn that clock!" and I flung myself over.

In the pitch black, I heard something move.

What was that?

I strained to hear over the blood throbbing in my ears. I forgot to swallow and clung onto the bed sheet so hard the bones in my fingers hurt.

There it is again!

I swiftly turned to face the far corner of the room.

It sounded as though something, or someone, was trying to crawl across the floorboards but couldn't get anywhere.

I dared not move or breathe.

Then, from the same corner of the room, there came the very faint sound of what I thought was a hornet.

I couldn't stand the dark any longer and, full of fear, I reached over and switched on my lamp.

I shuffled back onto my pillow, holding the sheet up to my chin, and scanned the room.

Nothing, and now no sounds.

I took a cautious look at the floor, peering at the far corner, and wondered whether or not to get out of bed and check.

"No, it's all fine."

Yet I didn't fall asleep until dawn, when I vaguely heard birdsong as I finally drifted off, and the resonant lowing of the few remaining cows from Mr Wilson's barn.

"Are you feeling all right, May? You look rather pale today."

I sat at the kitchen table with my head slumped. Aunt Celia leaned over and gently lifted my chin.

"You've hardly slept, just look at those rings."

"I couldn't get back to sleep," I said, looking at her half-concerned, half-annoyed face, through bleary eyes, "and I have such a headache. I do feel a bit under the weather today, Aunt."

"Well, you won't be in any fit state to do anything physical today, I suppose," she said, and resumed her reading of a recipe pamphlet. "So that means you won't be able to give a hand at the hall. If that's the case, you can help me with some light housework, surely that can't make your head any worse."

I made no reply but felt happier knowing I didn't have to spend my day with the villagers.

"You can sweep the floors and take the rugs out, the carpet beater is hanging on a hook in the cupboard under the stairs, in case you've forgotten. Meanwhile, I shall pay a visit to the Leadbetters' and offer some sort of apology on your behalf. Lord knows what explanation I can give, I hardly understand in the first place, but the longer it's left the worse it shall become. And clearly you're not in any form to see them yourself."

"Thank you, Aunt Celia."

"Just make sure you don't put me in this ghastly position again. I shall continue to be your guardian, naturally, but that doesn't mean you can take liberties. Just because you are my brother's daughter doesn't mean you can get away with murder."

Murder, now there's an idea.

I ate my bread and drank my milk, fantasising about Lizzie Leadbetter and what I would do to her.

But of course, I didn't mean it, not deep down.

After moving some of the furniture in the parlour and taking the big rug into the back garden, I quickly grew bored of housework. It had never been that way at home; I used to enjoy helping Mother around the house, she made it fun somehow, and silly. She felt house proud but knew there to be more to life than drudgery.

"A little bit of dust here and there isn't going to kill anyone. Let's leave the polishing for today and go see your dad, shall we? We can take him some of those biscuits we made, he'd like that."

I beat the carpet harder and harder, the clouds of dust swirling in front of my face, and I kept my mouth shut tight and eyes half closed.

The carpet beater creaked in my hand as I thrashed at the rug hanging on the line.

I took a step back and turned my face away. I felt hot and worn out and my head throbbed even more.

"Maybe she did this on purpose," I muttered, wiping sweat from my brow. "This is her way of punishing me after all."

I decided I had done enough and pulled the rug down. It was heavy and awkward to carry, so I dragged it over the grass and through the kitchen then back into the parlour.

I sighed.

"I forgot about that one."

Another fair-sized rug, underneath the piano, needed beating. I let go of the other, pulled back a chair from the small table, and fell on to it.

"However am I supposed to get that from under the piano?"

I sighed again.

The parlour felt cool and I closed my eyes, wishing away the pain in my head, but closing my eyes was the worst thing I could do; I became nauseous and my head swam and when I cautiously unscrewed my eyes, the light hurt.

"I can't do that rug, I just can't."

I slumped, staring at the piano. The longer I stared, the greater the urge became to play something – anything – just to be taken away from the world around me.

"Something gentle, though, a lullaby perhaps."

I sat on the stool, positioned my fingers over the keys and then changed my mind.

"No, let's try Mum and Dad's favourite, see if I can remember."

I re-positioned my fingers. They hovered for a few moments as my anxiety at perhaps having forgotten how to play "These Foolish Things" got the better of me. I didn't want to fail them.

Taking a deep breath, I started to play.

I smiled as my fingers travelled over the keys, as naturally as writing a letter, and with growing confidence I played harder, forgetting the pain in my head.

I hummed along, occasionally singing a line here or there, wincing when I hit a bum note at which point I'd have to start again.

As I became more and more wrapped inside the melody, images of Mum and Dad, dancing in our tiny sitting room, whirled around my mind. Mum's big grin and laughter as Dad held her close, and his shuffling feet on the dark red rug, those worn-out slippers tripping on the loose carpet threads.

My smile grew wider.

Baby June in the cot in the corner, standing up and clapping, as I played on the rickety upright piano in the window.

"You never knew where to look, did you? Me or them."

She would end up flicking her head from left to right, left to right, her big blue eyes taking it all in.

"And Father would lift you out…"

They would always end up dancing together, the three of them, while I played on, looking onto the quiet street, but forever craning my neck to see what was happening behind me.

"All so perfect."

I played the same song five times over, desperate to keep the happy thoughts on a loop, watching my parents dance again and again, until I believed everything I pictured had become real.

But the truth hit me in the throat. I opened my eyes and looked to the ceiling, trying to suppress any tears from falling, and I hammered down harder on the keys as if crushing my sadness to smithereens.

"Damn it! Damn it all!" I shouted, plunging down onto the keys. I pressed hard, the sound loud and despairing, but, reflected at me, in the shine of the polished piano, were a pair of hands I didn't recognise.

I froze and watched in horror as the hands mimicked my own. They had the same spread of my fingers, the same bending, the same crook of my right little finger, but they were not my own. They were big and strong, the fingers thick and long and crooked.

I couldn't believe what I saw; dark hairs grew along each finger, the nails – filthy and scuffed as they were – had been sharpened to points.

I began shaking. My hands trembled slightly but I tentatively started to play, and the hands in the reflection followed my every move.

I shunted back on my stool and slammed down the cover.

I ran from the house.

"What have I done?" I whispered, "What have I done?"

My legs were like jelly but I ran as fast and as far away as I could. I must've had some kind of instinct not to run for the fields because I found myself heading in the opposite direction, past the green and towards the train station.

Outside the butcher's, on Butchers Lane, stood a group of ladies with their baskets, but they soon stopped their gossiping and all turned to watch me as I ran by. I heard one laugh and another say, "There she goes again, she's almost feral, that girl." No doubt their gossip resumed but of a different sort.

I really couldn't care less. I felt such a terror that not even the threat of bombs dropping from the sky or of Hitler setting foot on our land could surpass.

And I knew – I *knew* – the reason.

"All of it, all of it…" I panted, the sweat dripping from my face, "it's all real! What have I done?!"

I ran along the lanes, the sun blazing down, my head burning with thoughts of demons.

"No, it can't be, it just can't be!" I cried out, pulling at my hair, "they're not real!" And in my mind's eye I saw the hands reflected at me, and I stumbled, falling to the road. I scuffed the heels of my hands and scraped holes in the knees of my blue trousers. I rolled over into a sitting position and held my hands to my face; pieces of stone were embedded in the skin and I sat, huddled up, staring at my shaking and bleeding palms.

"Mother… what did I do?"

How long I stayed in the baking sunshine, I couldn't tell, but if it hadn't been for Mr Wilson coming along in his truck and sounding his horn, I would have remained there for the rest of the day. As it was, the horn startled me, and I turned swiftly, expecting something else, something horrifying.

"What do you think you're doing, missy? Sitting in the middle of the road like that, are you barmy?"

I got to my feet but said nothing.

"May? Are you all right?" asked Mr Wilson. He was leaning out of his window and, when I looked up at him, his eyes grew wide.

"What have you done?" he asked, but his tone of voice seemed scared, rather than concerned.

"I tripped over, Mr Wilson," I managed to say, but with little conviction and turning my face from him.

He gave no reply.

I began walking past his truck, looking straight ahead. I heard him winding up his window and then the rev of the engine as he drove off. A black cloud of fuel-smoke gathered about me and I walked on, my mind completely blank.

"Where on Earth have you been, young lady? It's almost seven o'clock." My aunt stood in front of me, her hands on her hips.

"I went to the train station," I answered flatly.

"The train station? But why? What have you been doing there?"

"Just sitting, watching people come and go, watching the trains come and go."

I didn't want to be on my own. I'm so frightened, Aunt! Help me, please!

"Come into the kitchen, please. I must talk to you. I had a very unwelcome visit from Mr Wilson this afternoon with some strange tale about you sitting in the road. Go on, on you go, and sit down," and I was ushered into the kitchen.

I sat at the table, studying the cracks in the old oak wood, and pressed my sore hands together between my knees.

"Now then," Aunt began, pacing about the room, "is it true, about you sitting in the middle of the road?"

I cleared my throat, and quietly replied, "I tripped and fell, Aunt."

"That's one explanation and I shall give you the benefit of the doubt as I'm sure you wouldn't purposefully block the road. But something else Mr Wilson said..." Her tone changed. She didn't want to repeat whatever it was Mr Wilson had told her. "He seems to be under the impression that you, that you had perhaps... *killed* something, an animal."

There came a pause. I looked up at Aunt Celia, her face conveying a mite of fear and genuine worry that it could be true.

"Whatever made him tell you that? And no! No, I haven't killed anything!"

I was shocked into anger; why would Mr Wilson say such a thing?

My aunt sighed.

"But of course you wouldn't – I didn't believe it of you, May – but he did say you had... you had blood over you. On your blouse and hands, and some on your face."

"What? No!" I shook my head frantically. What was happening? Why would he lie like that? And then cold fear gripped me; *it must be, it's got to be...* I started to shake and then shouted, "You can see for yourself, Aunt, look at my clothes!" and I stood up, pulling at my blouse to show her the truth.

She scanned my top and trousers and her shoulders dropped slightly with relief.

"There, do you believe me?" My lips trembled, and I fought against bursting into tears.

"Now, May, calm yourself," Aunt Celia said, coming over to me. "The silly man made a mistake, that's all. I can see for myself – there's nothing on your clothes – except... what's that?" and she pointed to my knees.

"I tore my trousers when I fell down," I answered, rubbing the damaged material distractedly, "and I cut my hands."

I held up my palms and she made a face of displeasure.

"Yes, thank you, I can see," and she went over to the sink, "come along, May, they need a jolly good scrub," and she turned on the tap.

I did as I was told. She yanked on one of my arms, put my hand under the running water, and with the nail brush and coal tar soap, she roughly washed away the dirt.

"Mr Wilson probably meant the blood on your hands, ridiculous man, telling me you were covered in it," Aunt Celia muttered, cleaning my other palm. I looked at her profile and felt a rush of affection. I swallowed hard, trying not to cry; she had taken my side, she hadn't dismissed me at all... but I couldn't tell her of the horror that now followed me, how could I? Nobody could believe such a thing. My isolation smothered me.

I'm alone. No one can help me. What am I to do?!

"There, now dry them properly," and Celia handed me a tea towel. Again, I did as I was told.

"It seems I shall have to have words with Mr Wilson," Aunt went on, taking half a loaf from the bread bin, "he'll probably have told his wife, of course, and that will mean she'll pass it on to everyone else in the village." She began carving a slice, her face set for confrontation. "Well, there's nothing to be done for now, so we shall sleep on it."

"I'm so sorry, Aunt Celia."

"This isn't your fault, May, for a change," and she handed me the bread on a plate. "Now then, milk? Or there might be some tea left in the pot."

I lifted the teapot lid and peered inside.

"I'll have what's left, thank you."

I spread a thin layer of jam on my slice of bread and ate it slowly. My mind became full of dark figures; the man in the field, the strange shape in the tea leaves, the shadow, and now... those hands.

I swallowed but the bread stuck in my throat.

"May?"

I barely heard her.

"May? Whatever's the matter? You don't seem to be yourself."

I turned to her, desperate to speak of my anxiety, but said, "I'm fine, Aunt. It's probably just tiredness."

"Well then, I shall be off..."

"Where are you going?" I demanded. Panicked by her words, I shot straight out of my chair.

Aunt Celia jumped in surprise at my outburst.

"If you'll let me finish," she said, "I was about to say that I'll be off to the parlour now, I've got that knitting to be getting on with."

She gave me a confused look before leaving the kitchen.

I sat down, my heart thumping.

The parlour...

And I knew I would never play the piano again.

I didn't stay long in the kitchen. The thought of being alone terrified me, and after dashing upstairs for my notebook, I hurried after my aunt. I quietly pushed open the door to the parlour and poked my head round.

"Is it okay if I sit with you, Aunt?"

She stood by the cabinet and had just put on her glasses. She peered at me from over the top of them, looking surprised.

"If you wish to, May," she replied, turning her attention back to the cabinet. She crouched down, opened the small doors and pulled out her box of wool and rags. "Although I must say I never would've expected you to spend an evening with me, not out of choice, anyway," and she got up.

I didn't know what to say.

"Well don't just stand there," she said, with a small laugh. "Go and sit down."

I held my notebook tightly and made my way over to the round table. I barely lifted my eyes from the floor, not daring to see the piano, and I sat down, putting my book onto the lace cloth.

The clock marked out time from the mantelpiece and I heard it grow louder and louder. I slumped into my nightmare, unable to believe it was really happening yet fully aware of my mistake and its consequences. I shook my head, saying to myself, *no, no! This isn't real. It isn't real!*

"Is there anything you wish to tell me, May?"

I turned to her, still in a daze.

"No, Aunt. Why do you ask?"

She sat in one of the tall armchairs, a ball of wool by her feet, but her knitting needles and the blanket she worked on, rested in her lap.

"You are extremely quiet, more so than usual. I may not have a mother's instinct, but I am aware when people behave out of character."

My heart thumped.

Should I tell her? I want to tell her!

I gazed at her, hoping the neediness I felt could convey everything with one imploring look, and she would tell me I was just being silly, and everything will work out fine...

"Really, Aunt, there isn't anything wrong. I'm a little under the weather, that's all."

She resumed her knitting, eyebrows raised, "Well, if you say so."

She'd probably blow her top if I mentioned anything to do with superstitions, so how could I ever explain this?

I chewed on my bottom lip, thinking of everything Mum had ever told me, hoping some memory would give an answer, but there was nothing.

"There's got to be a way," I said under my breath, without realising.

"What was that?" Aunt Celia asked.

"Oh, oh, nothing," I answered, turning in my chair to face her, "I was just remembering something to write down, that's all."

I saw the piano and held my breath, waiting for the horror to show itself to me, but I hurriedly turned and faced the table again. I opened my notebook, pulled out the pencil from the spine, and started to write.

Monday evening, 23rd July

I've made a terrible, terrible mistake. It's all true, oh God, what have I done? Mother, what have I done?

Six

It was all I could write, my mind crushed by fear, and for the next hour I could do nothing at all.

"May, it's getting rather late," Aunt Celia announced, and I heard her get up from her chair. I jerked in my seat and quickly hunched over my notebook, hoping she would change her mind and sit back down again.

"It's time you went to bed," she said.

My heart grew small with panic.

"I'm in the middle of something," I lied, "can't I stay with you while I finish?"

The baffled silence hung heavy in the parlour until my aunt eventually replied, "What is this? Has my niece been replaced by another young girl made to look like her? Really, May, I would never have thought this of you, you're always so aloof."

I slowly turned to her. She stood by the piano, her hands full of knitting, and the surprise on her face made her glow with what could have been pleasure. She removed her glasses and rubbed the bridge of her nose.

"I know," I said, "and I'm sorry for that. I'm trying, Aunt, I really am."

Aunt Celia smiled at me and said, "I see that, May. You're not such a naughty thing, after all. Very well, I shall add a few more lines to this blanket and you may carry on with your writing. It's nice to see you occupied with something that doesn't involve tampering with fruit buns."

And she sat down, slipping her glasses back on. I watched her for a few seconds, realising that she had a well of emotions too; she just showed them in a different way.

I felt like crying as I turned back to my notebook. I had no intention of writing, but I had to make a pretence of it. And so I sat, terrified and frozen to the spot, trying to think of a way out. But it wasn't long before I was ushered upstairs to bed.

I entered my bedroom with trepidation. I poked the door open with my foot, reached for the light switch, and slowly walked in; had anything changed? Was there something in there, waiting?

My neat bed remained unaltered, the table beside it with my lamp and book also, the small wardrobe in the corner had both doors shut firmly, as I'd left them. The blackout had already been drawn and I went across to the window, lifting it slightly. Outside, in the darkening lane stood Mr Mason and Mr Roberts, both with their hands deep in their pockets. Mr Mason nodded at whatever Mr Roberts had said and they simultaneously looked up at my aunt's cottage. I dropped the corner of the blind and sat on my bed.

"They've been talking about me."

I reached across to my side table, placed my notebook onto it and then stared at the plain white wall.

"What have I done? What have I done?"

And I started to cry.

"How will I ever make it through tonight?" I whispered, my tears trickling onto my lips, "how can I ever go to sleep?"

"May?" suddenly came the stern voice of my aunt, and I held my breath. "Are you all right in there? I thought I heard something."

I swallowed before saying as cheerfully as I could, "Yes, I'm fine. Goodnight, Aunt Celia."

"Goodnight, May, see you in the morning," and the floorboards creaked as she made her way to bed.

Her words caused more tears.

"You might not see me in the morning, not if... Oh god, someone help me!"

I collapsed onto my bed sideways and silently cried until I could cry no more.

I woke in a state of panic and threw myself from the bed, frantically checking every corner of the room, but all appeared quiet and untouched. Birds were singing loudly from the hedges in the lane and I checked my watch.

"Quarter to seven, how long have I been sleeping?"

Having cried for hours, I had worn myself out and must've drifted off without remembering. I went to my washstand, poured out what little water remained into the bowl, and splashed my face. The mirror showed my eyes to be puffy and pink, and my skin appeared mottled and unhealthy.

"She's going to ask some awkward questions about this." I pinched my cheeks, trying to regain some colour.

I hurriedly got out of yesterday's clothes and pulled on a thin sweater and a pair of shorts. I then brushed my hair with quick, hard strokes before tying it up in a ponytail.

"She'll know," I told my reflection in the mirror. "How could she not, you look dreadful, but, really, that's the least of your worries right now."

I slowly drew back the blackout and looked upon the beautiful world outside. It knew nothing of my torment.

"I must get to town, I must, I must," I whispered, and then swiftly turned to my wardrobe. I fumbled about at the back of one of the shelves until my fingers closed round a tin that once contained mustard powder. "I must find the library, I've got to get..." and I pulled off the lid. "Oh no, it's gone! I shall have to ask Aunt... but she won't give me any money. What am I going to do?"

"May? Are you up?" came Aunt Celia's voice from right outside my bedroom door.

"Err, yes, yes I am," I called, and then hurriedly stuffed my empty tin back into the wardrobe. I had just closed the door when my aunt entered the room.

"Now..." she began, but stopped, obviously perplexed. "Whatever have you got the light on for?" she asked. "Turn it off immediately, I shall not have waste in this house, not of any kind."

"Yes, Aunt." I went to my bedside table and switched off the lamp. I then stood, twiddling my fingers, waiting for her to continue.

"As I was about to say, I have an early meeting this morning with a few ladies of the W.I., we agreed the earlier the better, so I shall be leaving the house in about an hour. After that, I have a few errands to run, and after *that*, I shall be calling at Mrs Cartwell's. There's to be a small gathering for tea and a discussion on roses. Apparently, Mr Roberts was at such a loss over the roses from the parlour, that he's organised an intimate meeting for the gardeners amongst us, and Mrs Cartwell has agreed to host. I think she enjoys making a fuss of people, dear thing. So, the day is essentially yours, May. I shall be out for hours and you may do as you please. It's pointless for me to ask you to do anything, but please, try not to upset any more of the villagers, will you?"

She was perfectly dressed in a navy-blue skirt and jacket and a white blouse. In her hands she held a small blue pillbox hat. The blouse had been buttoned all the way up to the top, but her gold cross hung modestly from her neck and trembled with every word expressed.

I stared at her, feeling as though I'd just met her for the first time. Everything about her seemed bright and free, her elegance shamed me, and I regretted everything I had done to provoke her. In my terror, I needed her to be my saviour and, seeing her so smart and unaffected, I felt a closeness I hadn't experienced for a long time.

I took a step towards her, and was about to open my mouth and beg for her help when she suddenly said, "Why don't you take yourself off for a picnic? I know how much you enjoy the fields about here. I could cut you some sandwiches and pack a bottle of lemonade, you could even pick some of the strawberries from the pots – they've grown rather plump – and then you can stay out all day if you wish to."

I gazed at my aunt with a surge of affection, but my heart grew heavier and heavier until I almost fell to my knees with the weight of it.

"May? Are you quite all right?"

I straightened up.

"Yes, thank you, Aunt. And thank you for such a lovely idea…" I paused, waiting for my courage to rise, "…but…

would it be possible for me to take a bus journey into the town? I had thought of paying a visit to the library."

"What a good idea. I expect you require the fare to take you into town, hmm?"

I breathed a sigh of relief.

"If that's not too much trouble, Aunt Celia."

"I think you deserve a trip away from the village. You seem to be trying these last couple of days and it may do you some good." Her voice became quieter as she called back, "Now let me just fetch my purse and we'll see what we can do."

"Thank you," I whispered, my shoulders slumping. "Thank you."

By ten o'clock that morning, I was on the number seven bus heading to Northampton.

I sat at the back with my knapsack and satchel, looking out on the passing countryside – already shimmering in the growing heat – and wished I had never been so childish. My stomach jangled with nerves and every time the bus bounced along the road I expected butterflies to be thrown up and out of my mouth. I couldn't sit still, constantly fidgeting and tugging at the sleeves of my thin top. I had to keep vigilant, I had to be aware of everything around me.

Apart from three ladies who sat talking together at the front, I was the only passenger. I kept my eye on the three women, jealous of their gossiping and breezy manner. I started to shake, and gripped onto the underside of my seat. I screwed my eyes shut as hard as I could, but their chirpy voices and laughter twisted the knife, reminding me of my own hellish desperation.

I became angry, hating those women. They were doing it on purpose. With gritted teeth, I opened my eyes and glared at them.

"Oh, my god…"

I couldn't help myself from hurriedly clambering onto the back seat, clutching my knees up to my chin, eyes fixed and wide.

"It's here," I whispered, my mouth hanging open. "It's here."

Next to the ladies there stood a dark figure, unmoving, and with its back to me. I watched in horror as the three women continued to chatter away, completely oblivious of the creature beside them.

The bus jolted. In that instant, bull horns flashed on top of the creature's head. I drew in a sharp breath and tried to climb up the back seat. Another jolt, and I clapped one hand across my mouth.

A body lay across its shoulders. Huge, coal-black arms were hooked around the knees and throat of its victim, but the image vanished as quickly as it appeared.

I could do nothing but stare, pressing myself against the back of the bus.

Leave me alone, please leave me alone!

Another jolt and I nearly screamed at the sight of the bloodied body, draped across its shoulders.

And the three women laughed.

Go away, go away. Just go away!

I couldn't take my eyes from it. Motionless and pitch-black, I knew it had all the time in the world.

At last the bus came to a stop. Passengers got on and greeted the three ladies.

In that moment, the demon disappeared.

Where's it gone?

I looked about wildly but it had vanished. My shock soon caught up with me, and I half-collapsed onto the back seat, juddering and shaking.

"'ere! Get your shoes off that seat!"

As I became aware of my surroundings, I saw all the passengers turn to look, while the bus driver leaned out of his cab, pointing his finger at me. I said nothing, but quickly gathered up my things and shunted across to the window seat, turning my face away.

"Kids these days, they've got no respect for anyone or anything," the driver said, loud enough for everyone to hear.

I vaguely heard the animated voices of the people on board, but quickly lost sight and sound of the real world.

Help me. Someone, please help me.

It took a lot of effort, stepping off the bus.

When I felt my legs were strong enough to hold me upright, I hurried onto the platform with my head down, avoiding eye contact with the driver. He told me off again, but I ignored his admonitions, my mind throbbing with fear.

Having reached the town centre, with the bright summer sun shining up at me from the cobbles of the market square, I suddenly felt lost. I stood for some moments, looking at the ground, before turning on the spot and studying the buildings all about me.

"I can't remember where it is," I muttered, half faint with the heat and my nightmare. I stumbled forward.

"Are you all right, duck?" a kind voice asked, and I turned to see an old lady reaching a hand for me. She had pure white hair, mostly hidden under a pale blue scarf, and her eyes were as bright blue as the sky. She smiled.

"Thank you," I answered, standing up straight, "it's just too hot, I can't bear it."

"Ooh, I know," she said, adjusting the knot underneath her chin. "Om never known such heat as this, not in all me years."

I cleared my throat and asked, "Would you be able to direct me to the library please? I'm not from Northampton and have only ever been in town twice before."

"Of course I can, me duck," and she took me by the hand and led me to the edge of the market square. She pulled me up and then pointed up a long, straight street. "Now, all you'm gotta do is foller-it right dane, keep gooing till you see the Notre Dame school on your left – you can't miss suthingk like that – and on the other side's the library."

She let go of my hand and smiled at me.

"Thank you very much," I said, and began walking up Abington Street.

"All right, ducky, you take care."

I stepped along the wide thoroughfare as if in a dream. Passers-by were faceless, they drifted past me in a distorted haze of hats and mouths, words spoken but all I could hear were high-pitched noises and squeals. Children ran and skipped and shouted, while mothers scolded them, dragging them back and smacking their legs. I walked on. A little red face looked up at me, his chubby cheeks stained with tears, while a mother's hanky roughly wiped them away. I turned slowly and crossed to the other side of the street.

By the time I reached the library, what little energy remained to me had almost been lost to the fearful sickness I felt.

I tripped up the steps. The darkness of the entrance felt wonderfully cool and I breathed it in.

When I entered the main room, my mind went blank After a minute's pause, a tall, grey-haired gentleman approached me, saying, "May I help you?"

I thought he'd called me by my name and I glanced at his face.

"I don't know you, do I?"

The man gave an expression of amusement and surprise.

"No, my dear," he said quietly, and with a small laugh. "You don't know me, but I saw you hesitating by the doors and wondered if you needed any assistance."

"Yes," I replied rather too quickly, "I would like some assistance, thank you."

"Follow me then, young lady," and he wandered over to the desk. He sat down and then smiled up at me. "Have you registered with us?"

"Oh, yes, here." I opened my satchel, fishing out my library card from the pocket and passing it to the librarian.

"May Meeson. And is this your first visit?" he asked, handing back my card.

"Yes," I said, "apart from the day I registered, I haven't been in this county for long, you see. I'm staying with my aunt in Guilsbridge. Do you know it?"

"Oh indeed I do, yes. Very handsome village, that. Now then, you've not come all this way to natter with an old man like me. What are you looking for today, Miss Meeson?"

His kindness upset me. I swallowed a couple of times and said, "It's a bit of an unusual request, I hope you don't think me strange for asking."

"Everyone who comes into this library is a little bit strange, including myself," and he winked. "Besides, anyone who wants to borrow a book from us is always welcome," and he leaned across his desk, "no matter what kind of book they're after."

I took a quick breath before saying, "In that case, could you direct me to any books you might have on superstitions, or that sort of thing, please?"

"Yes indeed." He stood up and led the way, turning to look over his shoulder. "Now, we must go to the deepest, darkest depths of the library for that kind of topic. Folklore and spiritualism."

I followed, not at all at ease with his comments.

"Here we are," and he stopped before a rack of shelves.

I thanked him, my heart beating a little faster. I scanned the book spines but couldn't focus on any titles.

"You're very welcome. And if there's anything else I can help you with, just pop to the desk and ask."

I nodded. When he had wandered out of sight, I hastily read book titles, but without order. I darted from shelf to shelf, up and down, across, pulling out copies before thrusting them back.

"I don't know what I'm looking for," I whispered, my panic rising. I glanced over my shoulder at the sound of footsteps on the floorboards. A boy with red hair vanished behind the children's section.

I began reading out titles.

"*It Moans on Land and Sea*, what's that? No, no good... *Quaint Old Customs of Wales*... *The Realm of Faerie, Fairy Life and Legend in Britain*... no, no, no." I moved up a shelf. "*British Goblins*... no... hang on, what's this? *Folklore, Old Customs and Superstitions in Shakespeare Land*."

I pulled out the book when another caught my eye.

"*Jewish Magic and Rituals*," I murmured, slowly putting back the other. I reached across and took hold of the dark blue spine. The lettering was gold. "*Jewish Magic and Rituals* by Herzl Rosenberg," I whispered, slowly stroking the plain front cover. "This could be it."

The book appeared new and unused, and inside the cover was printed the date, 1938, with no stamps.

"Nobody has ever borrowed this book," and I instantly felt some attachment, as though it had lain here waiting for me, and me alone.

I clutched the copy to my chest and then hurried over to a table by the window. One old man looked up and nodded before his attention returned to the large book spread open in front of him.

I quietly dumped my satchel and knapsack from my shoulder and onto the floor, and then pulled back a chair. I sat as closely as I could to the table-top and held the precious book up.

"Please work, please tell me I can fix this," I whispered and, before turning to the first page, I slowly scanned the library. I then opened my book and began to read.

...Isaac Lucia, 1534-72, and the transmigration of souls, or 'gilgul'. A process by which souls could continue with their journey to reach self-perfection. They would return by entering others in order to repeat tasks they had failed in previous lives, but Lucia's disciples became detached, promoting the belief of dybbuks being in possession of human beings. These dybbuks, or dybbukim (plural), had once themselves been human, but because of their sins they are forced to wander the realms restlessly until they discover the perfect resting place inside a living person...

...translation of dybbuk, 'cling,' or 'attachment'... the myth of Gehenna and the escape of dybbuks... some other scholars disagree and maintain the idea that the dybbukim were in actual fact rejected from Gehenna, their offences being too terrible to be accepted...

...the prophet, Elijah, possessed by the soul of a dead man who desired war and so wished to trick the King... Book of Samuel, the Old Testament, "And it came to pass on the morrow, that the evil spirit from God came upon Saul," but through the power of David's music, the terrible spirit was lured from inside King Saul...

I couldn't take it in fast enough, devouring the next line before reaching the end of the first, but I now knew what it was that I had invoked.

"Dybbuk," I whispered, looking up from my book. The library had become busier, a few people sat reading newspapers, and I hadn't noticed any of them, absorbed as I was in the terrible fascination of demons and spirits of the dead.

I stretched and yawned, shifting in my hard seat, before returning to the book

...if a dybbuk enters your body, it will, over time, possess you. You will gradually become what the dybbuk had once previously been in life. If the soul had, when alive, been a smoker, then the body it now lives in shall become a smoker. If the soul had been cruel and friendless, so shall the new host become, turning on family and friends until the dybbuk can live in its old and comfortable circumstances. In short, you will repeat the same sins and life choices the dybbuk did, when living.

My eye caught something on the opposite page.

To rid oneself of such a destructive soul, only a rabbi who has mastered practical kabbalah can perform such an exorcism. A group of ten men, called 'minyan', must gather around the afflicted person in a circle and pray. They must recite the words of psalm 91, three times, as the Rabbi blows the 'shofar' (rams horn) in a certain tone. The body of the victim is supposed to 'shatter', spiritually, allowing the dybbuk to be shaken out... the previous humanity of the dead soul is appealed to by the Rabbi, asking of it questions such as: what do you want from your host, why do you wish to remain here, and who were you in life? This is intended to appease the dybbuk, to relax it and so leave the host willingly...

"That's it," I muttered, leaning back in my chair, "it has to be."

My mind tripped over itself in relief, excitement, and terror. What if I couldn't have an exorcism? *What if I'm turned away?*

"I must ask where the synagogue is."

I checked the clock on the wall. It was coming up to midday.

"There's still time," and I gathered up my satchel and knapsack, still holding onto the book, and wandered over to the gentleman behind the desk.

"May I borrow this, please?" I asked quietly.

He looked up and reached across, smiling as he took the book from my grasp.

"Well now, what have we here?" And he drew it close to his face. I watched his eyebrows rise ever so slightly on reading the title, before he said, "Hm, this one has passed me by. So then, two weeks?" and he grabbed the rubber stamp, rolled it in ink, and then thumped down hard on the inside page.

He passed it to me, saying, "Interesting choice for a young lady," and he paused momentarily. "When you're done with it, I might give it a go myself." He offered a small smile before lowering his eyes.

"Of course," I said, understanding, "it's fascinating, really." I hesitated, half-turning, but then I leaned across his desk and whispered, "You don't happen to know where the local synagogue is, do you?"

He cast glances around the room.

"Yes, indeed I do," and he opened a drawer. With a sheet of paper and a pencil, he quickly drew a rough map and slid it across the table-top.

"Why do you need to know?" he asked, looking impressed and worried at the same time.

"Oh, it's nothing really. Just a personal project I'm working on. My mother's family were once…"

"I know," he said, smiling. "Well, good luck, May Meeson. And see you return that book on the dot."

I nodded, feeling a small flutter of hope, and then I left, stepping out of the darkness and into the blinding light of a summer's day.

Seven

Overstone Road, a long row of terraced houses and shoe factories. Some women had come out from work, their hair tied up and hidden with brightly coloured scarves, and all smoked nonchalantly on cigarettes. They looked so pretty, chatting and laughing in the sunshine – and I wished to be grown-up, like them.

As I continued, I nodded at the occasional housekeeper who had come to sit on their front steps, a cup of something in their hands. They nodded back.

"Afternoon, duck," they each said.

"Hello," I replied, keeping my head down and hurrying onwards.

I stopped and looked ahead, shielding my eyes with my hands, and saw a large, corrugated-iron building.

"That must be it," and I reached for the map the librarian had drawn for me. On it he had written: *former Jerusalem Temple, you can't miss it, great ugly thing it is*.

I looked up and suddenly became apprehensive. I had no idea what to do – I didn't know anything about rules and what could cause offence – I didn't even know if I was allowed in, there could be restrictions.

I chewed my thumb and eventually told myself I had absolutely no choice, so walked on, entering the huge shadow cast by the synagogue.

Almost immediately, the doors were opened and a man, dressed in a black suit and prayer shawl, stepped out.

"My goodness," he said, "you startled me," and he put a hand to his heart.

"I'm very sorry, I didn't mean to make you jump… err, am I allowed to go in? I need to ask the advice of a rabbi."

The gentleman seemed quite taken aback and began gently pulling on his short white beard.

"You need advice for why?" he asked, still tugging his beard. He gazed at me with soft brown eyes, clearly pondering my appearance and perhaps even my soul.

"I have some questions… about, well, how can I put it?" I felt stupid, and his unfaltering gaze made me feel like a child.

"Has it anything to do with food?" he asked.

"No," I said, perplexed, "not at all."

"Ah, well," he said, stepping closer and taking me by the shoulders, "it should be. I'm just on my way to have some lunch on the Racecourse. Why don't you come along with me and tell me your trouble? I may even see my way in sharing what little food I have with you." He smiled and his whole face became wrinkled with laughter lines.

"That's very kind but…"

"No buts," he said, letting go of me. "You've piqued my curiosity. Why should a young English lady wish to speak with a rabbi? Especially one who, to my recollection, has never been to this synagogue before. Perhaps she is an evacuee from London and wishes to join. Perhaps she is Jewish... Perhaps she isn't. Either way, you've made me very curious indeed... and yes, I am a rabbi. My name is Josiah Sachs, or Joe Sykes to those who don't like being reminded of my background. Now, shall we?"

He gestured that I should lead on, and I did, completely bewildered by him. He walked next to me on the roadside, as a gentleman should, and lowered his head. He pulled on his beard again, apparently thinking deeply, before turning his face to me and asking, "So what is your name?"

"May, May Meeson."

He nodded several times.

"That is your father's name. And your mother's?"

"Well," I began, beginning to feel ashamed, although the shame was not my own, "it should have been Spenadl, but my mother's family changed it years ago... to Spencer."

"Ha!" and he nodded again, a smile on his face.

"They were religious, a long time ago," I started to explain, "but my mother wasn't, and she barely mentioned it."

We were heading the opposite way from town and, after crossing the road and passing more terraced houses, we eventually came out onto a park. Tall beech trees lined the outskirts and shimmered in the sunlight, their leaves rustling gently in the warm breeze.

"Now then," he said at last, directing me to a park bench. I sat down. He looked at me kindly, still smiling. "What is your trouble, May?"

"But how do you know I have trouble?"

"Let's see..." and he groaned slightly as he sat on the bench. He pulled out a brown paper bag from each of his jacket pockets and placed them in his lap. "First, you were standing outside the synagogue, and not many people hang about there unless they need something or wish to insult me, and you didn't insult me. Secondly, I could see your feelings of desperation – do not take offence – it just means I could tell you had something on your mind that worries you. Thirdly," and at this point he began unwrapping his paper bags, "you told me you wanted a rabbi, and not many people want a rabbi unless they are getting married, planning a burial or want an exorcism of some kind. Your little face told me it wasn't the first, so it is either a burial or an exorcism. And both of these things are very troubling, so I assume you have troubles."

He peered inside one of the paper bags and made a face of dismay.

"Fish paste... again. Would you like one?" and he offered up the bag. I had completely forgotten about my knapsack, and said, "Thank you very much," and delved a hand into the bag, pulling out half a sandwich.

"My pleasure, but sadly not yours." He held up his own half, turning it around. "You haven't tasted it yet."

I took a small bite and chewed slowly, wondering how to begin explaining my nightmare. Josiah Sachs munched his sandwich in silence, patiently waiting for me to speak.

"I don't want you to think I'm being silly, or even worse, lying."

Josiah nodded and brushed breadcrumbs from his lap.

"I've just come from the library," I went on, and reaching into my bag. I pulled out the book and passed it to him. Josiah took hold of it.

"Interesting," he said quietly, and then looked across at me. "What is it about this book you wish to discuss with a rabbi?"

I put down what remained of my sandwich onto the armrest of the bench, and then shifted in my seat to face him.

81

"Something has…" I sighed and started again "…I think I've done something I shouldn't have, or didn't do something that I should've done – a thing that I've always done, throughout my life – but once, just once, I decided against it."

The rabbi pinched his chin, eyebrows knitted together, and my library book held to his chest

"What did you *not* do?"

I cleared my throat as my tummy turned to jelly.

"Please don't think I'm insane when you hear this."

Josiah didn't say anything.

"Okay," I said, taking in a deep breath, "you see, I was brought up on superstitions, and, one day, I wished I was dead." I swallowed as my mouth became drier. "And I sneezed on it."

I took a quick look at the rabbi, before continuing, "Well, Mother used to tell me if anyone sneezes while people are talking of death or illness, then everyone must pull their left earlobes, three times. And it's what I've always done, only…"

"Only this time you didn't?"

"No… I don't understand though, how could English superstitions be effective against anything that's Jewish?"

"Why would our cultural divisions influence deeper, more fundamental forces?" he asked. "There is truth to be found in many belief systems, and superstitions are often a distillation of what people have found works best. For example, tossing spilled salt over your left shoulder, you know that one?

I nodded.

"That comes from Buddhism. We have a habit of acquiring such things in this country, and adopting them as our own." He smiled. "Now, what has happened?"

I looked up to the treetops. "I think I've invoked something, a spirit or demon, maybe a… a dybbuk, I don't know. But it's real, and I'm terrified."

"How has this demon shown itself to you?" The rabbi's voice had lowered, and he barely moved his lips when he spoke.

I breathed a sigh of relief. He believed me.

"Um, the first time was on the horizon, in a field. And it must have had something bright in its hand, because there was a flash of light and it made me jump. The next time I guess was as a shadow, at home... and the same night it appeared in my tealeaves. Then, that night, I heard strange sounds in my bedroom, I'm not sure if that has anything to do with it, though. The next time I was playing the piano, and a pair of huge hands were reflected at me. On the bus today, I saw it standing next to a group of ladies."

The rabbi shifted on the bench and I stopped talking.

"Now," he said, lightly placing a hand on my shoulder, "can you describe it to me? As much detail as you can."

I trembled just thinking about it.

"Well, it's very dark, but I don't know if it's robes of some kind. I've not seen a face, but it's tall, and sometimes I get the impression it has bullhorns..."

The rabbi suddenly let go of my shoulder.

"Sorry," he quickly said, shaking his head, "please continue."

"The hands are very big with long fingers which are quite scuffed. But the nails are very sharp... err, I can't really say much more than that... other than, at times, I think he's carrying something, someone, across his shoulders."

I suddenly shivered as a cool wind blew, and goosebumps prickled on my legs.

The rabbi stared ahead. I looked at him with a sense of trepidation.

"Rabbi?"

He hung his head slightly and took in a deep breath.

"May…" he began, turning to face me, but he abruptly stopped. His eyes grew wide and his lower jaw dropped.

"Rabbi?" I asked, feeling sick with nerves. "What is it? What's the matter?"

He was looking beyond me, and I turned. I couldn't see anything.

"Has anyone ever seen you and believed you to be covered in blood?" he asked, his voice barely audible.

"Yes," I replied, "Mr Wilson accused me of killing an animal, that was only yesterday… but how do you know about that?"

Josiah swallowed, still unable to look me in the eye.

"This creature of yours, this is no dybbuk."

"What do you mean? What is it then?"

He couldn't speak.

"Rabbi, what is it? What are you seeing? Tell me! Please!"

I swung around in my seat, searching for the demon, but still I couldn't see it anywhere. The breeze picked up, blowing colder, and I rubbed my arms.

"A dybbuk," he said slowly, "was a human being first. The creature who follows you has no name – ancient – and this one has an attachment to your family, someone many years ago must've done something very wrong, perhaps meddled in dark arts, for it to pursue your name so long. And waiting," he whispered to himself, still staring at the same spot with wide eyes. "It's waited a long time." He drifted off for a minute, eventually muttering, "I never thought that I'd actually *see*…"

I didn't understand what he told me.

"But, surely, you can get rid of it? An exorcism? I need your help, Rabbi, please!"

The rabbi suddenly looked into my eyes and said, "This was never human, it has never been a human being, there is no way of exorcising it."

"But there must be!" I shouted, jumping to my feet and pacing in front of him, "there has to be a way of getting rid of it! There just has to be!" I flung myself at his feet and cried, "Please tell me there's some other way, I'm so scared."

The rabbi cupped the back of my head and I started to cry.

"Listen to me," and I looked into his eyes. They were desperate. "There is one way to rid yourself of this creature, only one."

I swallowed, hardly daring to breathe. The rabbi let go of the back of my head, placing his hands in his lap.

"But," he whispered, "we have to leave this place. We must leave now," and he quickly got to his feet, stuffing his paper bags back into his pockets. "Come, hurry, I have to get you away from here."

He lifted me up, casting a furtive glance across his shoulder. I followed his gaze.

"What have you seen? Is there something in that tree?" I asked, but he shook his head.

"Come, come with me," was all he said, picking up my satchel and knapsack.

"Are we going to the synagogue?"

"No!" he practically shouted, but quickly regained his composure, "Sorry, May, no. I shall take you to my home."

He gently pushed me ahead, his head bowed, and we walked. I couldn't help myself and took one more look at the tree by the bench.

"It's here," Josiah said, quietly. "Don't look. Keep walking, I'm with you now."

"What will it do to me, Josiah?" I asked in a shaky voice. Everything was shaking – my body, my vision, everything around me – and I hardly knew how I managed to put one foot in front of the other.

Josiah walked beside me, putting an arm across my shoulders. He gripped onto my arm tightly and leaned his head close to mine.

"We will get to my house, I shall make us some tea, and then we will talk. But not now, not here."

And we swiftly went on. But for the rabbi's firm grasp, keeping me upright, I wouldn't have made it to the end of the path before falling.

The rabbi's house was dark when we entered; the front door had only a small window at the top, and barely any light fell through to the short passageway.

Josiah gently propelled me to the left, through a doorway, and into a tiny sitting room. I stood, swaying slightly, as he moved across to the window and pulled back the curtains.

"I hardly ever open them, seems pointless these days," he said as daylight flooded the small room.

I looked about in a daze; there stood a little square table in the centre, a thick red velvet cloth thrown over it, with papers, plates and crumbs scattered; a two-seater sofa was set up against the back wall, masses of manuscripts stacked upon the blankets covering it, and a modest bookcase nestled between the sofa and the green-tiled fireplace.

I stepped further inside and then looked over to Josiah, who stood watching me from the window. I couldn't see his face properly, backlit as he was, but he leaned on the back of a chair.

"Please," he said, "sit wherever you wish. I shall tidy away the things on the table and bring in some tea," and he came towards me. "May, sit before you fall, please."

I nodded and pulled up a chair at the table. I leaned my elbows on the throw, feeling the hard breadcrumbs dig into my skin, and then rested my head in my hands. I heard Josiah shuffling about as he tidied away the papers and brushed the crumbs onto the floor. And then suddenly I heard the rattle of a teacup on its saucer as it was handed to me.

"Here, drink this."

I lifted my head and then sat back in the chair.

"I'm so sorry for this," I said, trying not to cry again, "I am so, so sorry to come to you with my troubles, it isn't fair on you…"

"Now stop that," he said, sitting opposite me, "I am here for a reason…"

I smiled weakly.

"…why do you smile?" he asked.

"Oh, nothing. It was something my mum used to say, 'everything happens for a reason', you just reminded me for a moment."

"She must've been a person of wisdom," he said quietly, and I nodded before I felt my face crease and I burst into tears.

"She was the one who told me what to do, the spitting over the left shoulder, the tugging on the left ear lobe," I cried, "but she never explained *why* I should be doing it."

Josiah leaned across to me and took hold of my hand.

"You cannot blame your mother, she probably had no idea either. The truth of the reason has probably been lost over the course of generations." He sighed. "It's likely something that was simply drummed into her, as a religion.

Once these things get into your mind set, it's extremely difficult to stop doing them."

I looked him in the eye.

"Except for me, of course," I said, pulling my hand from him and wiping my face.

The rabbi ignored my comment and instead took a sip of his tea.

"Listen to me," he said after a minute, getting up from his seat. "I shall tell you how to rid yourself of this creature…"

"Tell me!" I cried, my hot eyes gazing at him.

"Hang on, May. What I am about to tell you is not something I can approve of – I shouldn't be telling you at all – but…"

"Then why tell me? If you don't approve?"

Fear made me argumentative. I couldn't stop myself from snapping at the only human being who was willing to help me. Thankfully, Josiah understood, and took no offence at my outburst. Instead, he went over to his bookcase and pulled out a large volume, and then sat back down at the table.

"Now then," he began, turning the pages, "I am looking for a certain chapter."

I watched him in silence.

"Right, here we are," and he glanced at me. "Now this tells us how to handle a creature such as yours but, as I said, I cannot approve of such actions. I can inform you, but ultimately it is down to you and your conscience. You have the decision to make. Do you understand?"

I nodded. I could feel my heart racing and my breathing had quickened. I was dizzy with hope.

Josiah gave a few shallow nods in return. He sighed before turning once more to the book.

From outside, I heard voices and I looked over involuntarily, as two people passed by the window. I looked to Josiah who continued to read, his lips moving, but he didn't speak.

I clung to the seat of my chair, wishing for him to hurry and tell me what I needed to do.

Patience, he's doing all he can.

Someone else must've approached the house from directly across the street. The room became dingy as a figure pressed against the glass. I glanced up and instantly shunted back in my chair.

"What's wrong?" Josiah asked, startled by my sudden movement.

"It's at the window."

As I stared in horror, Josiah slowly turned to face the glass.

"My..." I heard him mutter, before the book he held clattered to the floor.

It leaned forward, bending from its full height, and watched us with white eyes.

"Don't move," Josiah whispered to me. "It can't harm you yet. Stay still and look away. Do not look at it!"

But I couldn't help myself. It was hypnotic, and it leaned in closer.

There came a terrific squealing, causing both of us to put our hands to our ears.

"Don't look at it, May!" I heard Josiah shout again, as the piercing sound of the demon's bullhorns drawing patterns on the glass sent electrical shocks along my spine.

"What's it doing?" I screamed, pressing my hands harder over my ears. Josiah shouted something back, but it was muffled, and I screwed my eyes up, wishing and wishing for an end.

The awful sound ceased abruptly. I gained the courage to open one eye and saw the sunlight through the window. I breathed a sigh, but not of relief, and the rabbi and I looked at one another, both exhausted.

"What was that about, Josiah?" I panted, at last. He bent down and retrieved his book, shakily opening it and placing it on the table.

"It's the next stage," he said, putting his head in his hands and massaging his forehead. "There are many stages it has to go through before it can reach you completely. You described to me the shadow and the reflection. The image of you covered in blood is what it wants to do to you, and, I am sorry to tell you, much worse."

"How many stages are there?" I whispered. My entire body had turned ice-cold at his words.

"There are many, but this is nearing the end." He looked down at his lap.

"But," I stuttered, "what's next, then? And how soon?"

"It's impossible to say when, but…" he tailed off, not wanting to reveal the truth of my nightmare.

"Go ahead, tell me, I have to know."

"May, according to the book, there are only two stages left. And they are both physical. Once it has achieved them, it will take you."

For the first time, I felt some sort of calmness. Here were the facts, this is what it was, and this is what I had to deal with.

"Okay," I said, "What do you mean by physical and how do I stop it?"

Josiah stood up and paced about the room. He muttered to himself and from the odd word I caught, he suddenly seemed struck by the reality of what he had encountered.

"Rabbi?" I asked, but he didn't hear. "Rabbi?" I called again, louder. But still he talked to himself. I got up from my seat and went across to him.

"Rabbi, please!" I begged, grabbing him by the wrists. He seemed surprised to see me.

"Oh, I'm so sorry, May. It's simply that I never thought that I would…"

"See something like this?"

He looked into my eyes and I saw shame in them.

"Yes, May. But it's selfish of me to be thinking of it in this way. You came to me for help, and I shall tell you what I know."

We left the house at about four o'clock. I had my book. Inside were a couple of pieces of paper on which I'd hastily written notes as the rabbi detailed the ritual that needed to be performed.

It had been hard for Josiah; he wanted to help me, as he wanted to help everyone, but he knew by telling me these things it would put someone else in danger.

He walked me to the bus station, making sure I understood all that he had said.

"It isn't something I can condone, May. You see that, don't you?"

And I did see, but I didn't need his approval to survive. I wanted to live, and I didn't care how or what I had to do in order to be rid of my demon.

"Life isn't fair," I said to him as we waited, "I understand that. It isn't fair that I should be hunted by some creature I know nothing about, and it's not fair that the factory exploded and killed my family, or that thousands of men are being blown up because of one man's insanity. Nothing in this world is fair."

I think he saw me differently after I said all that. But, again, I didn't care. All I wanted was life.

And, secretly, I'd already made up my mind.

"I cannot wish you luck," he told me, as the bus pulled up alongside us, "I shall be praying for you, whatever decision you make."

But he must have known what I was already planning.

After I stepped onto the platform and handed the driver my ticket, I turned and smiled at Josiah.

"Thank you, for everything. I'm sorry I involved you in this, but I had no choice, nobody else could've helped me."

I sat at the back of the bus and waved to him as we drove away from the station. He waved back with a look of tremulous pity and guilt across his face.

"Two stages," I muttered, and I fixed my mind on Lizzie Leadbetter. "Two stages left."

Eight

As I waited at the stile, shaking with fear that she wouldn't turn up on time, I pulled on the knot of my neck scarf. I gently rubbed my throat and winced in pain, but I needed the air to soothe my skin.

The demon had come to me that night, after my meeting with Josiah. It had hunted me in my dreams and hadn't allowed me to wake until it had scarred me.

I stared at the yellow grass of the field, remembering pieces of the nightmare – the images fragmented and brief, but horrific – and my shaking increased. I remembered how it had held me by the throat, and how its touch burned like fire, searing my skin. I saw the eyes of glowing white, so hypnotic and full of hatred, devouring my soul with the intensity of its imminent revenge.

I paced about in the long grass, clapping my hands rapidly out of sheer nervousness, and shook my head from side to side.

"No," I whispered, "no, it won't get me. She'll be here, she *will* be here."

I looked to my watch and then back along the hedgerow leading to the village.

"Come on, for God's sake!" I muttered, clenching my fists. Time was getting on.

The fear made me sick, and all I could do was pace about, my gaze never leaving the hedgerow in hope of seeing Lizzie Leadbetter strolling along towards me.

And then I had a jolt of panic that I had forgotten something, and I undid the pouch from my belt. I pulled it open.

"You've got everything on the list, you've checked again and again. It's all here." And then I quickly checked the pockets of my dress. I felt my aunt's compact mirror – the lid of which I'd unscrewed and removed the night before – and then carefully held onto the small pocket knife I'd taken from the garden shed.

"It's all here, everything is here."

I shot a look up.

"Only *she* isn't."

I checked my watch again.

"Three ten," I whispered, sickness surging through me. "If she doesn't get here soon, I think I shall go mad."

I'd paid Lizzie a visit the previous evening, asking for her kindness and compassion. I flattered her in the most absurd manner, gushing with admiration. I acted like a fawning, pathetic little girl who only behaved so abominably because I was jealous of Lizzie and her talents and her prettiness. I sobbed a little, for my own faults, and wished to be like her.

It nearly didn't work. She gave me a sneer and the look of someone who knew the game I was playing because she herself had played it many times before.

I persevered – I had no choice – but toned down my desperation to please her.

"Look," I'd said, as she was about to close the door in my face, "I know what I did to you was horrible, and I'm truly sorry. And I understand if you don't want to be friends, but you could at least do me the courtesy of accepting a gift?"

She'd faltered at the word, 'gift', and my heart fluttered. I went on.

"Please try and understand how difficult it is for the new girl to fit in, especially when you're so mature and have such style, it makes me feel like a child, and I lashed out at you. And I know it isn't your fault that I have no family, I'm just so envious of what you have. I'm sorry, Lizzie, would you please accept my apology? If not in words, then in the form of a present? I went to town yesterday with only one thing on my mind – to make it up to you. I spent most of my savings on…"

But I clammed up. Lizzie's eyes sparkled, and I thanked the stars that she was so predictable.

"On what?" she'd asked, her curiosity growing, and opening the front door a bit wider.

"Oh," I'd said, bashfully, taking a step down from her door, "no, I can't say. I want it to be a surprise. I want to see your face when you see it for the first time…"

I heard my voice gaily continue with the lies, but in my mind I was seeing the field, the demon, Lizzie and the blood all over the grass.

She'd leaned on the doorframe, becoming more relaxed as the thought of an expensive gift softened her spite.

"Well, where is it?" she'd asked.

"Just meet me tomorrow, at the stile, at three-fifteen."

Her face had crumpled with displeasure.

"Please," I'd urged a little too desperately, "I thought if we were to try and become at least polite to one another, if not friends, then maybe we could have a kind of picnic? Aunt Celia gave me the go-ahead, and she says she will make us some sandwiches, and jam tarts, and even give us a bottle of lemonade she's been saving for a special occasion."

I patted myself on the back with that one; I knew full well she couldn't refuse me after mentioning my aunt and her role in the 'picnic' because, if she did, *she* would be the one who would appear ungrateful and unkind, and that wasn't part of her act.

"Fine, I shall be at the stile at a quarter-past three." With that, she'd slowly closed the door.

As I remembered the whole episode, I gave a smile; I knew exactly what she was thinking, that she would turn up, take the present, and then leave me all alone, maybe even laughing as she went.

"Oh no you won't," I muttered, searching the hedgerow for any sign of her. "You won't be going anywhere."

I checked my watch again. Three-fourteen. My stomach fell away from me and the sickness throbbed upwards.

"Come on, come on… hang on… Who's that?"

As I looked back up and towards the village, I saw a flutter of pink skirts and long, tanned limbs, as someone came around the bend of the hedge.

I squinted.

"It's her! She's come!"

I nearly jumped up and down with relief, but quickly regained some sort of composure. I couldn't let her see my agitation; she was smart, and it wouldn't take much for her to change her mind and leave.

"Just keep her here for another ten minutes, be nice, give her some lemonade and chat away gaily, as if nothing matters," I said to myself while watching the arrogant sway of her hips as she walked. I gritted my teeth.

"Well, here I am then," she announced, flicking her long hair over her shoulder with the back of her hand, "and I'm on time. How long have you been here?"

"Oh, only about five minutes," I lied. "Look, I've laid out the blanket and set up the picnic already."

I watched her give a well-practiced look of indifference, but in her eyes I could tell she approved. She was greedy, and the raspberry tarts and bowl of strawberries looked pretty and inviting.

"Hmm, yes I can see," she said casually, stepping over the stile and making herself comfortable on the rug. "Can you pour me some of that lemonade? Walking has made me thirsty."

I ignored her deliberate rudeness and, crouching down, opened the bottle and poured out some of Aunt's homemade lemonade. My hand shook but thankfully, she wasn't looking; she sat on her side, leaning on one hand, and scanned the countryside. The gentle breeze ruffled her hair slightly, and she wore the expression of a model posing for a photographer. It was all I could do to not burst out laughing and call her a stupid cow.

"Here you are, Lizzie," I said in the tone of a public-school slave and handing her the teacup.

"Mmm," was all she could muster as she snatched it from me. I checked my watch furtively.

Three-eighteen.

After draining her lemonade, she cast her eye over the picnic, and then reached for a jam tart without asking. She slowly, and daintily, ate the pastry.

You stupid, stupid cow.

97

My stomach churned, and I felt for the mirror and knife in my pockets.

"So where is this gift you promised me?" she asked after finishing her second jam tart. She had done well not to show her eagerness for it.

"Oh, I thought we should enjoy the picnic first, and then I will give you the present," I stammered, checking my watch once more.

Three twenty-three, come on, only another few minutes.

I could see her annoyance; her cheeks flushed, and she quickly got to her feet, dusting down her pink skirt.

"Look, you promised me a real apology, but if you've got me here under some childish false pretence, then I shall leave immediately."

"No," I cried, scrambling to me feet, "you can't leave, not yet."

"Why not?" she demanded, and then laughed. "My God, you really are pathetic, aren't you?" and she laughed again.

"I *have* got something for you, Lizzie, I really have," I spoke quietly. I hated her, how I *hated* her.

"I don't believe you, you're a little liar, and I shall tell everyone in the village how much of a fibber you are. That and how you're such a weed – having to make things up in order to gain friends – pathetic."

She turned her back on me as if to climb onto the stile, when she stopped and turned to face me.

"And I shall tell you something else; your parents ought to have been ashamed, bringing something like you into the world. No fight, no spirit, no manners, no *class*. If I was anything like *you*, I'd apologise to everyone I met for being so dreary."

My heart thumped harder and harder. I looked at my watch.

Three twenty-nine. Nearly there, another couple of minutes.

"You have absolutely no style," Lizzie went on, warming to the task now. "Just look at the state of you. What *is* that you're wearing? Your grandmother's old bathroom curtains? Awful, even for the war…"

She continued with her abuse and mocking, but I had stopped listening. I slowly turned to face the horizon, and the young oak tree in the hedgerow.

"But I have got something for you," I said again, quietly. I heard her scoff.

"Where is it then?"

"Here," and I undid the pouch from my belt. I faced her, holding the drawstring of the leather bag, and then offered it to her.

She made a face, sneering and snorting, and snatched the pouch from me.

I slowly put my hands back into the pockets of my dress, and held onto the mirror and knife, holding them so tightly it hurt.

I closed my eyes briefly, breathing calmly, and then looked again at the horizon.

"What *is* this?" I heard Lizzie's baffled voice say.

"Inside that pouch," I said softly, "is a small amount of earth that I had to collect from this field. You'll also find some of my nail and hair clippings, and a piece of cloth soaked with my blood and saliva, along with my mother's tortoiseshell pen – it was the only thing I had left of her family – and there are some jasmine flower heads somewhere in there, too. I don't really understand what they're for, though…"

I heard her gasp.

Three thirty-four.

I quickly drew out the mirror and held it up to the sky. The sun caught the glass, and, from the horizon, there came a flash of lightning in response. I suddenly turned to Lizzie, the pocket knife in my other hand.

She wore an expression of absolute disgust and shock, so much so that she barely registered the bright light beaming from across the field.

"This is my gift to you, Lizzie."

She looked into my eyes, her own eyes now conveying a terror of me, and tried to say something but I didn't give her a chance.

I slashed a curve into her bare arm and then stumbled backwards, staring at the blood as it began to seep.

Lizzie, mute, held onto her bleeding arm, the string of the pouch caught round her fingers.

"Take her, then," I started to shout, "I've done it! Take her!"

The sky grew dark. The gentle wind turned harder and stronger. It whipped about the blanket, rattling plates and teacups.

"Take her, then!" I screamed, looking to the field for the demon.

And there he stood, his dark arms reaching out for its victim.

I pushed the stunned girl aside and jumped over the stile. I cowered, hiding behind the post; I had no idea what was about to happen.

The wind pulled at our clothes and there came a terrific screeching; it filled the world, growing higher in pitch as the wind began dragging Lizzie away, and she finally found her voice.

"Help me!" she begged, clinging onto the wooden fence. "Help me, May! Please!"

The demon's call became deafening, sucking in the air around us, and I closed my eyes, putting my hands over my ears, huddling down as far as I could.

Yet I could still hear her pleas.

"May! What have you done to me?!"

I took a quick look, only to see her being ripped from the fence, her fingers snapping as she desperately tried to hold on.

I had never seen such fear on a face before, and I scrunched my eyes up tightly, wishing and wishing for it to come to an end, but time seemed to have stopped.

Eventually, her wailing grew distant, and the wind began to ease. I stood up and cautiously opened my eyes.

The long yellow grass of the field bowed and waved in the breeze. I let my gaze wander further, hoping the demon and Lizzie had already vanished to another world.

It was wrong to hope.

He stood taller than before, arms holding Lizzie aloft like a prize, and I watched, dumbfounded, as there came a rainbow of blood, erupting all at once from her side.

Her screaming echoed inside my head, and I fell forward onto the fence, the sickness surging out. My entire body shook uncontrollably, and the only thought I had was, *that was meant for me! That could've been me!*

As I wiped my mouth, gasping for air, I couldn't help being drawn back to the terror.

Lizzie, motionless but alive – I could still hear her crying – lay across its shoulders, the huge arms pinning her in place.

"It should've been me," I whispered, blinking as another flash of light beamed across the field, but it soon began to fade.

It had taken less than a minute for the demon, with Lizzie pinned across his shoulders, to completely disappear.

I didn't move for quite some time. I felt exhausted and without emotion, seeing beyond what lay in front of me.

"It should've been me," I repeated, not feeling anything. "It should've been me."

"So, did you and the Leadbetter girl have a nice time?" Aunt Celia asked when I returned home. She was washing a small bowl of potatoes in the kitchen sink as I stepped in through the back door.

I had the picnic basket, and the neatly folded blanket tucked under my arm, and I gave my aunt a smile.

"Yes, thank you, Aunt Celia, we both had a lovely few hours together. I'm sorry I ever played that horrible trick on her, she's actually a very nice girl."

I put the basket on the table and began unpacking the contents.

"Oh, I am pleased," Aunt Celia said. Turning to face me, she added, "You're becoming quite a mature young lady, I must say. I'm so glad to see this change in you."

She turned back to and resumed washing the potatoes. "Supper won't be ready until six, I'm afraid," she called over her shoulder.

"That's fine, Aunt, I don't think I could face eating anything for a while, anyway."

"Did you walk back together? You might've invited her in to join us for a little supper, I can always make things stretch for friends."

I said nothing.

"May?"

"Oh, no," I said, feeling the mirror and knife in my pockets. "She said she was going to meet someone after the picnic. I don't know who, but the way she spoke I'm guessing it was a boy."

"Oh, really?" my aunt said in a disapproving tone. "Does her mother know?"

"I couldn't say, Aunt."

"I see. Well, I hope you don't get any ideas about boys, May. I'm sure your mother and father would say the same thing."

I smiled sadly, remembering Albert Pensey and the lie I'd told Mum.

"Now, would you care to pick some mint from the garden please, May?"

"Of course," and I wandered into the back garden.

Different varieties of mint grew alongside the old wall, where the jasmine spread its creamy flowers and beautiful scent. I stood and looked at it for a while, thinking.

"You did it," I whispered, absent-mindedly rubbing the edge of the knife in my pocket, "you won."

The relief and reality hit hard, and I doubled over in tears, sobbing as quietly as I could when I really wanted to wail and scream.

I crumpled up on the grass and thanked the heavens that I had survived.

"May! Wherever is that mint?" Aunt Celia called from the kitchen door. I wiped my face hurriedly.

"I'm... I'm just coming," I called back in a quiet voice. I pulled out my knife. The blade had the merest stain of blood, which I wiped on the ground before cutting off five sprigs of mint.

"I should think so, madam," came my aunt's almost jovial voice. "We shall all be dead of hunger if you take much longer."

My hands – one holding the mint, the other the knife – were shaking uncontrollably. And then I suddenly sneezed.

'We shall all be dead...'

My breath caught in my throat and I dropped both the mint and the pocket-knife. I looked up to the sky, hastily pulling my left ear lobe three times.

"Never again, Mother," I promised, the tears falling down my cheeks, and I squeezed my eyes shut against the horror. "Never again."

"May! Really, whatever are you doing out there?"

I gathered up the mint and hid the knife in my pocket.

"Coming, Mum," I muttered, and, a little unsteady, I got to my feet.

About the Author

Emma Coleman is from Northampton and, for that reason alone, supports the local football team, the Cobblers. She spends most days negotiating peace treaties between her four cats, none of whom like each other very much. Apart from football and demented cats, her other loves include collecting early edition H.E. Bates, nature, and local music legends, Bauhaus. She also fancies pigeons.

NP NOVELLAS

An exciting new series of high calibre fiction in concentrated narratives from some of the most accomplished writers around.

#1: Universal Language – Tim Major (April 2021)

An intriguing murder mystery that pays homage to Asimov's seminal robot stories and also to the classic detective tale.

Investigator Abbey Oma is dispatched to a remote and failing Martian colony tasked with solving the murder of scientist Jerem Ferrer. The killing took place in an airlock-sealed lab, and the only possible culprit is a robot incapable of harming humans...

#2: Worldshifter – Paul Di Filippo (April 2021)

A high-octane tale reminiscent of Jack Vance at his best in its sweep and imagination, but wholly Di Filippo in its execution. When lowly shipbreaker Klom stumbles upon an active organic stasis pod deep within the bowels of a derelict ship, little does he imagine the deadly danger it represents. Klom is forced into a desperate chase across the stars as the most powerful beings in the galaxy determine to claim the secrets he has unwittingly discovered.

#3: May Day – Emma Coleman (May 2021)

Abruptly orphaned during wartime, May is forced to move to the country to live with her strict church-going aunt, who never approved of May's mum nor her heathen ways. Despite Aunt Celia's disapproval, May continues to practice the superstitions her mum drummed into her, until the one time she doesn't, at which point something dark arises and proceeds to invade her life...

www.newconpress.co.uk